Now That I'm Dead

A. Lee Bruno

"The Mind Is Everything"

Buddha

Consciousness cannot be explained by neuroscience or how the brain works. The data storage and processing capability required for the common functions of human consciousness require far more capacity than what we can observe in the human body. The discovery of microtubules and phosphorous atoms in cells and their apparent association with the body's cell coherence offered particle physicists new theories that worked under the principles of quantum mechanics. They assert that human consciousness may expand beyond the brain as an extension of wave-particle duality common to subatomic particles. In which case, consciousness may continue after death.
https://www.outerplaces.com/science/item/4518-physicists-claim-that-consciousness-lives-in-quantum-state-after-death
https://www.scientificamerican.com/article/what-happens-to-consciousness-when-we-die/

ACKNOWLEDGMENTS

Thanks to my beta readers whose enthusiasm for this book encouraged me to move forward.

Mary
Pamela
Margaret
Marsha
Deborah

CHAPTER 1

I awaken to the feel of 800-thread-count sheets against my feet. This simple luxury was mine by way of my daughters' guilt for putting me in the Potomac Gardens Assisted Living Center. Likewise, the "private suite" that overlooks the rose garden, but still harbors that institutional smell of cafeteria food and disinfectant.

The May sun shines into my closed eyes as my mind climbs reluctantly above the fog of sleep. Waking up without incentives gets harder each slowly passing day. Ah, the roses should be peaking this morning, the roses on the other side of the windows that never open to the fresh air, never share the roses' scent, never let me forget I occupy a warehouse for used-up old farts. And this is a Sunday. On Sunday, the staff always brings The Washington Post with breakfast. I stretch, smile, and open my eyes in anticipation of Starbucks coffee and a slow, deliberate read of each section of the paper.

I raise myself up to see the roses better. Plop! What's that strange noise? It sounds like one of those big soap bubbles bursting—the kind that kids make with large plastic wands. How odd. I look around to see where the noise came from and there I am! Down below me. Lying on the bed, one bare foot and leg exposed, my head on the pillow, mouth open, my hair all bed-heady on one side, and arms out-flung.

The rest of the room rotates into view. Now I am looking down on the loveseat and coffee table where I usually take my breakfast. What's going on? I reach out, but can't feel the limbs that I just stretched a second ago. I can't seem to move or call out! Is this a dream? Wake up! Wake up!

My vision lurches as the room spins around. At that moment, Dennis comes in with the breakfast tray and newspaper. That's better. Dennis will put things right. The room stops spinning and I try to get his attention. Look up here! Dennis, here! By this time, a bluish tint is slowly moving up my foot. I note that the me in bed isn't breathing at about the same time that Dennis sets the tray down, picks up the phone, and punches two numbers. "Gina, it's Dennis. I think Fiona may be dead."

There I am, lying on my expensive sheets, exhibits of whiskers on my upper lip. Damn, I hate people seeing me like this. The sunshine on my face makes the white hairs on my mustache literally glow. No! Dennis, you're wrong. I'm not dead! I can think and see things, so I can't be dead. How could I be dead and so upset about what I look like? After all, there is no afterlife. Is there?

My mind ticks furiously through the research I had done in my thirties for a paper defending atheism. The books describing Jesus the Nazarene's time with the Essenes, the translations and articles on the Gnostic Gospels, the articles by famous physicists—waves of page after page of print with garish striations of day-glow highlights pass through my head. I read each white-out pocked page of my paper again, checking the citations, confident that I know this. There is no afterlife. But the blue tint is moving further up my exposed leg.

My arms are now turning bluish and I have to admit, I sure look dead. Jesus Christ! My atheist ass is so screwed!

Before the thought fully registers, the scene changes to the kitchen in my house—the house where I lived before the unfortunate kitchen fire that paved my way into Potomac Gardens. My beloved kitchen is now full of strangers pulling food out of my fridge. I'm in someone else's home now! How embarrassing!

Now I'm in the magnolia tree in the backyard. It looks the same and the waxy green leaves hide me well. I feel safer here as I collect myself. A soft noise from inside the trees sounds like small rubber balls being pushed through a tight place—bump, bump, squeak, bump. I hear birdsong, at first faint but getting loud then louder still. Oww! Then the sound adjusts to where I liked it before my hearing loss. Traffic noise from the highway and the TV playing inside the house are familiar, comforting sounds. My panic eases.

The sun shines as the soft May breezes rattle the leaves of the big tree. I wonder what I can see from the top of the tree? Shit! I'm now at the top of the tree looking out across the back fields that were once a horse pasture. On the rise overlooking the pasture is the old ramshackle tobacco barn overgrown with that damn Virginia creeper and wild grapes combo that dogged every day of my life as a gardener.

Hmmm. I think there for I go back to my spot under the leaves to clear my head and figure out what is going on. I can see and hear. I can think. I feel neither pain nor anything at all disagreeable, really. I just . . . am.

There doesn't seem to be anything of me to see other than a dim light. The only sound from me is a slight buzzing noise. Steady and consistent. Like an old fluorescent light fixture. Can I feel anything? I know that it was cool under the leaves, but I can't say that I actually felt the coolness. Let me see if I can tell any difference at the top of the tree in the sun. Whoosh! Back to the top. Hard to get used to this. Here in the sun it is warmer—two degrees Celsius at least. Damn. I'm using the metric system. That's not from memory!

So, what are the possibilities based on what I know? One, I am delusional, possibly a chemical-based delusion? Someone gave me a drug? Nah. Potomac Gardens doesn't have the spunk to knock off one of its residents. Then what? I woke up and bam, everything changed. Or maybe I never woke up. This is a bizarre dream. Or I had some sort of spontaneous brain aneurysm, or a blood clot that damaged my brain. Regardless of how it happened, all of this has to be in my head.

"Or, you are dead."

"Who said that? Is that God? Can you hear me? Let me explain. I honestly gave Your godliness a lot of thought and it just didn't make sense given the mess You made of the Bible. I figured that if You were omnipotent and the Bible was meant to teach people how You wanted them to live, it would have been written more clearly." Get a grip, Fiona. You're babbling.

"Yes, I can hear your thoughts, but I'm not God. Sorry to disappoint. You can call me Jonas. I'm also dead and hang out around here. Couldn't help picking up your telepaths. You're projecting at full volume. Relax and your volume will drop. You never know who may be passing by."

"So there are lots of dead people around here?"

"About what you would expect for a quiet suburb of a big city. Dead selves generally go where they feel safe, so they gravitate toward their former homes; this is a major D.C. suburb. But, as you are learning, we can teleport to any place that we can remember or visualize. And since bad people die as well, it is always good to be cautious, especially when you are new at this. As you apparently are. May I assume that you are from around here?"

"I planted this tree when I moved here back in 1984—thirty years, six months, twenty-four days, eighteen hours, and forty-nine minutes ago. So, who's in charge of the dead selves?"

"You mean like a God type? No one that I can tell. We are on our own. At death, we kept our consciousness—intellect, memories, and personality—in the form of an AtCon—short for atomic configuration. That's your body now and all you need once you learn your way around."

"Whew! No offense if you're religious, but that is the best news I've had today. Of course, I apparently died today. Where are you? Can I see you?"

"Sure. But only dead selves can see AtCons. Look down and to the left."

"I see something about the size of a soccer ball that glows. You're much bigger than me."

"You can adjust your size by just thinking it. I have found this to be a good, all-purpose size that works in normal social situations and defends against accidental encounters with birds and wormholes."

"When did you die?"

"November 1864, when slaves were freed in Maryland. My owner tied me up and beat me to death rather than see me go free."

"Jesus Christ! How horrible!" Shit, I can't believe I said that. I have got to get my shit together. "You're a former slave? How come you don't sound like a slave?"

"Well first off, I don't 'sound' like anything since we're communicating by mental telepathy—I'm sending you my thoughts mentally. Would you feel better if I did this? 'How do Massa! Kin I get you sumptin? How about a lil song? De Camptown ladies . . .'"

"Well, I see that you are also a jerk. An insensitive, immature, and corny jerk at that. Did you die like that or is that something you cultivated after death? I've only been dead for 18 minutes and 23 seconds. Cut me some slack.

"Tell me more about being dead for 150 years. And by the way, condolences for your loss."

"Not 150 years—149 years, six months, nineteen days, nine hours, and thirty-eight minutes to be exact. No condolences necessary. Compared to my life as a slave, this is a vast improvement."

"But a horrific way to die."

"Yes, John Demerson—renowned tobacco grower, ladies' man, and card player—was one mean, nasty sonofabitch. See that walnut grove over there where that ramshackle old barn is? That's where it happened. My cabin was made of walnut logs and sat just on this side of the slope below where the barn sits. Demerson wanted me close enough to come when he rang the bell but out of sight so he didn't have to look at my black skin and ragged clothes. When Lincoln freed the slaves in the Confederate states in 1863, John saw the writing on the wall and sold my family off while he could still get top dollar. I never knew where they went. I stayed near this cabin after I died in hopes that my wife and three children would come here when they died. I always hoped that our last home together would be the safe place they sought when the fright of death panicked them. But they are long dead and there has been no sign of them."

"So, what you been up to these past 149 years, six months, nineteen days, nine hours, and thirty-eight minutes? Damn, I wish I could stop doing that!"

"I know what you mean. For reasons I can't fathom, dead selves are hung up on precise metrics. You'll get used to it after about four months, sixteen days, five hours, and twenty-three seconds. But to your question, at first I sat around planning revenge, but since dead selves have no physical form, we can't interact with the natural world. I could hover right over Demerson's head, but couldn't hurt him. The frustration was torture.

"Some of the dead play back their happy memories. Death leaves us with all our memories, as clear as the instant they occurred. Living in your past can be addictive if you have enough happy memories. I didn't. Then, one day I saw some children going off to school. These were happy little white children, skipping along full of play. It was like watching puppies. Then I took to following them to school, curious about what they did there. Over time, I learned the alphabet and how to read. Just by watching and listening and doing lessons in my head. The first time I ever felt powerful was when I read a letter written to the teacher from her father. Marks on white paper revealed what this white man said to her.

"From that point on, I read and learned from books and teachers. I kept up with classes at the University of Maryland until 1990 when computers came in. PCs speeded up learning for everyone and made it hard for me to keep up."

"'Cause you had no hands or fingers to operate a PC?"

"No. Don't have to. You can make your AtCon so small that you can go between the pages and use your optic sensors to record each page. Then you have it in your memory store where you can access it just like a computer. But when everyone could do it, I lost my competitive advantage. Up till that time, I had completed all the course requirements for mechanical engineering, architecture, agriculture, American history, literature, and political science. I listened to all the lectures and class discussions, wrote the papers in my head and then compared them and my answers to exams to the ones the teacher graded. I still stay in the main library most of the time, even now. Just reading interesting books. The more information you have, the more you can do. For example, I went to Paris by finding its coordinates on a map of Europe, concentrated on them, and in a flash I was on a rooftop in Paris. I could see the Eiffel Tower, the River Seine. I love Paris.

"Well, I have to go. Things to do before the ballgame tonight. The Nationals are playing a double-header against the Red Sox."

"Wait! What about the bad dead selves?"

"Stay in the tree, but enlarge your AtCon. Enjoy some favorite memories. Smell the magnolias, get some sun—you get energy from light—and sleep tonight. AtCons reboot when you sleep. I'll check back with you tomorrow. Ciao."

"So how do I keep from falling out of the tree while I am asleep?" No answer. He had just disappeared.

It is now 11:46 a.m. (EST) on May 19, 2014. What to do? I'm dead and wrong about the afterlife. How do Christians and Muslims take this? Must be a shock given their expectations. But we are all in the same boat, so if Jonas can get along for all that time, I can too. Let's see what else is here with me. First, I will think a bigger me. Ugh. Soccer ball-sized is too big for me to move easily through this tree. Softball-sized would serve me better. Down through the branches, hovering the way Jonas must have done around Demerson's head. The magnolia blooms are just starting to open and their smell fills my mind Or is that me just remembering the smell? Does it really matter? I am enjoying the scent. I progress down limb by limb. Along the way a squirrel runs up the trunk. Each hair is super high definition. Wow. It must have a nest up there somewhere. Finally, I'm on my favorite limb under the leaves. Amazing, without bodies there is no hunger, material needs, or way to cause physical harm. Or is there? How do I protect this glowy AtCon thing? And from what? What would happen if I flew into a power line? I have a lot to learn, but I can read books and ask other dead selves. I can do this if Jonas can.

"Izzat a request for help? Otherwise, I would not protrude on your thoughts. It's clear that you don't know from telepathy protocols, so I gotta ask. My name is Kittamaquund Wicomico of the Piscataway tribe. Most dead selves call me Kit Wico—at least the polite ones do. And I'm in zat magnolia blossom right below you. Here, I'll enlarge my AtCon. Dere. Can you see me?"

7

"Yes. Is this your tree? I'm Fiona Campbell and newly deceased." Geeze, that sounds so creepy. I'm about to weird out.

"Indians have no concept of ownership o' nature, which is how we were flummoxed outta our land. I was just passing t'rough and thought you might be Jonas. He hangs around here mopin' over his lost family. You're welcome to make this your restin' place, but you might prefer something with climate control. Just sayin'. If lightnin' strikes the tree while you're there?—pssssst! Your AtCon's electrons, protons, and neutrons—poof!—into the atmosphere. Me? I hang out around the Redskins' training facilities or in a VIP box at FedEx Field."

"You're a Redskins fan? Me too. Wait. So you're not offended by the name?"

"Nah. I remember when dey were the Boston Redskins. Back den we had a lotta sports teams with Indian names. Made us all feel remembered. Now I'm just confused. Of all the things done to us, to make a fuss about a name given to honor Indian strength and courage is distractin' from the more serious wrongs. No, my big beef with the Redskins is their win-loss record! No honor to our name if dey keep losing. Makes me mad every time I think of it. I remember when the 'Skins were fierce competitors. Loved to watch the games back then. Really reminded me of my live self days. But I digress. You had questions. Here you go, kiddo. I just telepathed answers to your questions and some info on telepath protocols to your memory store."

"Thanks. Any other advice for me?"

"Work your AtCon if you want to do well in this life. You know. Think, learn, create, do. Take me for instance. I died in 1624 a gamblin' fool. So I up and learned how to play and win at every form of gamblin' since den. I was up and down the coast from Jersey shore to Atlantic City. Now I'm on top of the games in the new casinos around here. 'Course, I can't actually play without a body, but I can bet on the outcomes of games of chance with other dead selves. Yeah, I have an addiction blah, blah, blah. And I indulge it mentally and get the same high as I did when I was alive. If you want to have a life after death, you have to work what ya got—the AtCon. Ain't that a bitch? No such thing as a free ride.

"Hey, enjoy your tree today. Weather will be clear, so no worries. Look for me in Suite 101 if ya wanta watch the Redskins in style. Oh, yeah, tell Jonas the same and I'll catch him next time I'm nearby. I sense a sore loser bearing down. Bye!"

Kit disappears just as Jonas had. That must be how teleporting looks to an observer—simply disappearing into thin air. And to think—I can do that. So much to process and it is still morning.

Let's see how my dead memory store works. There's a blur of colors and sounds but nothing recognizable. Slow down. Pick a specific event. Hot grease spilled on my arm and gave me that scar. Ouch. Mother holding me crying because she had spilled the grease on me. Sniff. A poopy diaper and air blowing through my hair. All of it recorded like a high-definition technicolor movie in my head. I fast-forward through a blur of scenes—me mopping floors, folding laundry, studying, sitting in traffic, and arguing with my daughters. Unfortunately, I'm not finding many memories that I'd enjoy reliving. Did I have to work so hard all the time? Or was it just easier than dealing with people who all seemed to universally disapprove of me, including my snooty kids? The way I talked, my unsolicited opinions, my temper, and sharp tongue— anyone can see by the looks on their faces that I was not very popular.

Sigh. Death, it seems, is a private rabbit hole tailored to match each one's personal baggage. Like Jonas, I don't have that many happy memories to keep me long occupied. And if I could have been different, I would have. Or did I figure on death being the easiest end to pervasive disappointment? At least a natural death is politically correct. Did that much right. But, the joke's on me. No telling how long this gig will run. What are my options but to try and make the best of it?

Everyone dies, but how many find their way out of the rabbit hole?

NOW THAT I'M DEAD

CHAPTER 2

I must have fallen asleep because I don't remember anything else until right before sunrise when the birds started a birdsong smackdown. Just as Kit said, my AtCon remained suspended in space, but not in time. The clock ticks just like it should. I know 'cause something just told me that it was 7:33 a.m.(EST) May 20, 2014.

"Hey! How did your first twenty-three hours, fifteen minutes, and thirty seconds as a dead self go?" Jonas was back.

"Not bad. I met Kit Wico who came by to see you and passed along the telepath protocols to my memory store. So, here goes. Fiona Campbell requests permission to speak and be heard as a friend."

"Jonas accepts you as a friend and invites you to speak and be heard. Now we are able to engage each other through the medium of mental telepathy with a level of safety because our AtCons will recognize each other. To send a message to another without their permission can go down as a social faux pas or the message could automatically be rejected. Comprende?

What did you think of Kit?"

"Seems like a nice guy, but like you, not what I was expecting. People are so old—from other times. It is amazing that they all sound like, well, regular people. How was the baseball game?"

"Same as all baseball games—a boring recitation of statistics; however, the lights during the night games make the air alive with electrons and I get a kind of buzz going. Closest thing to whiskey that I can get now. The place is full of dead selves high as a kite jostling into each other and falling off the top rung of seats."

"How do you tell one from another at the game?"

"Through our telepathic protocols, I can at least distinguish familiar minds from strangers from a distance. When we're out as a group like last night, we stay in our AtCons to avoid embarrassment. If we want to reveal our gender, we can project a picture or use holograms to simulate movement. Here, I will show you. Here is a picture of my wife, Israel."

"I see her! She is very pretty. Is the baby she's holding yours?"

"No, just a sickly baby of our neighbor who was out in the fields setting out tobacco plants. Israel baked bread for the big house and kept the baby with her, out of the sun. Israel always smelled like fresh bread. Always was soft in the heart for the little ones."

"Show me what you look like. Can you do that? Send me a picture of you?"

"Yes, and it can move like a hologram."

Sitting on the next limb appears a dark-skinned man with a compact build. He's wearing blue jeans, a western styled vest but no shirt, Stetson hat, and hand-tooled red cowboy boots. He is smooth shaven, has regular features but a scar across one eyebrow. His smile is crooked, like only half his mouth moves. His teeth are white and even. His lips are full and add a note of sensuousness to the sinister, crooked smile. But his eyes crinkle and they are cornflower blue!

"Wow! I didn't see the cowboy outfit coming. Those boots would get you killed in some D.C. neighborhoods. Very nice. I guess you moved on from your slave persona."

"About 130 years, eleven months, twenty-nine days, fourteen hours, and ten minutes ago. Got into the cowboy thing just recently—in the 1950s. Loved John Russell in the TV show The Lawman. But Paul Newman in the Butch Cassidy and Sundance Kid blew me away. The boots I saw in a magazine ad for Marlboro cigarettes. Like to never found a red pair that had the workmanship I wanted. Demerson had a saddle made of hand-tooled red leather. I never saw anything to equal it until I saw the boots in the ad. I got the boots to celebrate the end of Demerson."

"So you created a hologram that has Paul Newman's blue eyes and a fancy pair of boots? This is not what YOU look like?"

"I look like this except for the blue eyes. I made one small modification. That's nothing compared to what women do. Once the moving pictures got popular, every woman looked like the latest movie star. Clone after clone of Mary Pickford, then they all looked like Jane Russell or Marilyn Monroe. It got so bad that I forgot what a real woman looked like. So let's see your hologram! Show me a real woman."

"I don't know how. Do I just get the picture in my mind and concentrate on it?"

"If you want it to move and be three-dimensional, you should imagine yourself doing something."

"OK. Let me go back to when I was younger. That counts as me doesn't it?"

"Sure. Go for your best year."

"I think I will imagine me when I rode bikes with my daughters in Rock Creek Park in the 70s. I was in my mid-thirties then and denim was big. Am I doing it? I have brown hair and I'm wearing my favorite cut-offs and a green t-shirt. Can you see me?"

"Oh yeah. I can see you. You look healthy! Like, milk-fed. Your face is flushed and a sheen of sweat is on your arms and legs. Nice legs, lady. Not much for fancy clothes, are you? Take a break and sit down in your hologram and tell me your name."

"My name is Fiona Campbell, born white and hillbilly in West Virginia in 1938. I'm going to wave at you. Woohoo! Damn. My hologram fell apart. Riding the bike may have been too ambitious."

"You don't sound like a hillbilly."

"Well first off, I don't 'sound' like anything since we are communicating by telepathy—I am sending you my thoughts mentally. Would you feel better if I did this? How-dee! I'm right proud to be hyar, a-sittin and a-whittlin'. Let me git my banjo and we'uns can sing my Grand Ole Opry favorites."

"Touché. Had that coming."

"I left West Virginia for Pittsburgh when I was 16. Never went back."

I got rid of most of my twang. Embarrassed my kids when they were teens."

"What was in Pittsburgh?"

"Closest big city with jobs and enough people to swallow me up. I worked as a typist and was fast. Lived in the YWCA for a while. Took a test to get my high school diploma and then took the federal civil service exam. I took it enough times that I finally passed the test for a GS-4 position. But while I was waiting for a chance for a federal job, I got pregnant.

"Eddie and I married and he joined the Army to provide for us. Then I got pregnant again. Two little girls and a husband whose greatest ambition was a job in the steel mills. I really tried to make a go of it as a steelworker's wife, but I just did not love him. When the baby was two, I got a job as a secretary with the U.S. Marshals Service while Eddie sowed his wild oats. His cheating gave me the out I was looking for. After reading an article that said D.C. was the best place for blacks and women to work, I asked my boss to help me get something in D.C. He came through and I packed up my ancient Rambler with all our clothes and me and the kids came to Washington."

"Where you lived your dream of public service. Tell me, how is your ambition of some bureaucrat's secretary more lofty than Eddie's job at the steel mill?" Jonas was starting to sound a tad snarky.

"Not my ambition, but a stepping-stone. Birth control pills made college and a career possible. I could work and go to school as long as I knew there would be no more pregnancies."

"And is that how it turned out?"

"Damn straight, that's how it turned out. When I retired, I was a GS-15 and had a degree in Public Administration. And both my daughters went to college and are now married to lawyers. And now that I'm dead, they will inherit about $78,456.33 left in my investment portfolio."

"Speaking of being dead, any plans?" Jonas asked.

"Maybe I'll take a page out of your book and go learn all the things I never had time or money enough to learn. Or maybe I will

14

just read novels. Or go to baseball games and get drunk. What about football games? Now that I'm dead, I can go watch the Redskins live at FedEx Field in Kit Wico's suite. Say! That's something to really look forward to!"

"Be prepared for a crowd. The Indian dead selves around here love the Redskins too. They say that football and hockey remind them of games they played back in the day."

"You know, Jonas, all of this sounds a bit too good to be true. What's the downside?

"There is evil here in the form of dead selves who enjoy others' suffering. Although there is no physical body to torture, they look for ways to control your memories—find those that are painful and make you watch them over and over. They can only do that if they gain access to your memories by merging with you and you would have to agree to permit that. They can't do it against your will."

"Why would someone agree to be so vulnerable? What would motivate someone to take that risk?"

"Love. Sex. Curiosity. Loneliness. And/or a belief that the other person can be trusted. Dead or alive, people are people."

"You can have sex here?"

"In a way. Sort of. Just like you can enjoy your favorite pie. You can remember it bite by bite. How it looks, feels in your mouth, smells, and tastes. Every time I see someone eat chocolate I am reminded that will forever be an experience that I will never have. Once you die, your sensory memories end. You can't relive what you never experienced.

"I'm headed over to the University of Maryland library. Want to come along and catch up on your reading? The library is a big place and hardly used any more. Come check it out."

"Sure! I know where it is. Shall we meet at the main entrance?" Since you disappeared, I take that's a yes.

NOW THAT I'M DEAD

CHAPTER 3

"Know what, Jonas? It's been three weeks, four days, eighteen hours, six minutes and twenty-three seconds since I died and I have not missed my daughters at all. Shouldn't I feel their loss? "

"That's because you know right where they are and can see them anytime you want. You visited them, right?" Jonas' hologram was stretched out on a leather sofa in the microfiche archives, which is never visited, especially at 7:01 p.m. on a Saturday night.

"Just once. It was pretty boring, but I noticed that now that I'm dead, I see things that I never noticed before. Like Margaret is a helicopter mom and driving my granddaughters crazy. Sara's husband never makes eye contact with her, even when they are facing each other and talking. His eyes shift to just over her head or to the side. He's hiding something."

"Or he doesn't like her. Eye contact is a pretty intimate exchange." Jonas appears right next to me in my Fiona hologram curled up in a chair. He leans his face close to mine. "Especially when the eyes are Paul Newman blue." He bats his eye lashes furiously. I cannot help myself. I start laughing but my hologram doesn't move. That's funny as well. Now both of us are laughing and I am making those same snorting noises I made when I was alive.

"What's with the snorting? You can telepath a snort?" Jonas does not miss a thing.

"I confess. I was a snorter as a live self. It used to embarrass me so much but trying to stifle a snort when you are laughing hysterically can produce even worse noises. Yes. It's either a snort or a fart."

"The day you can telepath a fart, I will do somersaults in full hologram on the Mall." Jonas was now in convulsions of laughter. Damn, his hologram looked real.

My hologram is gone along with my composure when I sense danger. My AtCon, teleports up to the ceiling behind a cornice at the same time a bluish light moves across the room toward Jonas. "Jonas, danger at three o'clock."

"It's okay. These are friends of mine. Come on down and practice setting up your telepath protocols."

The large shadow are four AtCons arranged close together. As we come closer I pick up a telepath.

"I am Vince, and this is my son, Vince Junior. We are two of the pod known as Geeks Anonymous."

"I am Fiona and I accept you as an acquaintance. Speak and be heard."

"And I am Victor, pod leader of the Geeks Anonymous."

"I am Fiona and accept you as an acquaintance. Speak and be heard."

"I am Valiant, the Greek geek and new to the pod."

"I am Fiona and accept you as an acquaintance. Speak and be heard."

Jonas telepaths only me to say, "You can wait until all of them identify themselves to you and say just once for all four, "I am Fiona blah blah blah. That'll save some time. If you want to telepath all of them at the same time, project more than you normally do for one—like twice as much energy. Just think 'twice as much energy.'"

"What do you do to talk to a crowd of people?"

"We don't talk to large numbers at one time. Our AtCons aren't strong enough to send messages to more than four of five receivers at a time."

I addressed the four and Jonas, doubling my energy. "You are my first friends er acquaintances as a new dead self. I am pleased to make your acquaintance and hope you can tell me more about yourselves. What is a pod?"

Vince Senior answered, "Are you always so formal? God, Jonas, not only is she a twit, she's also a drag."

One of the AtCons was vibrating more than the others. I assumed it was Vince Senior's. "Really?? Well, the lot of you can just piss off if you can't show some manners. There's no call to act like that. I'm having second thoughts about allowing you telepath privileges!"

"Sorry, Fiona. Vince Junior here. My dad is now and has always been rude and overbearing. He treats us the same way as he treats you. We tolerate him because he is a brilliant but deranged computer wizard. He was part of the crew that designed the first computer prototype back during World War II. The Americans were slightly behind the Brits, but everyone was working on it at the same time. He died just as the big mainframes that he helped create were coming into their own and received no recognition for either accomplishment. Made him a little bitter. As for me, I died nineteen years, six months, three weeks, four days, and six hours ago, just as personal computers were expanding. I made a fortune before the IT bubble burst. Victor died after being instrumental in applying computer technology to operation of automobiles, household appliances, weapons, and medical instruments."

I sensed a telepath from Victor. "Valiant and I are the newest dead geeks and the most attuned to the current state of the art in computer designs and software. Both Vince Junior and I made fortunes writing new software programs. Valiant, on the other hand, was a master hacker and can make computers from odd scraps lying around the house. Unfortunately, he's a bit quirky. Like, he isn't actually Greek but his latest thing is alliteration, so he just uses words for the alliterative effect with no regard for their meaning. Yes, we know that telepathy negates the idea of alliterative speech, but we can't explain that to Valiant."

"The Vinces and I have been working on some way to communicate with the living. We can tour every piece of the most advanced computers, read every 0 and 1 in the software codes, but we cannot turn on or manipulate a computer. So we turned to radio signals—trying to use our AtCons to affect radio signals. We are making some progress in that area, but Valiant's interest lags and it takes one of us to mind him so he doesn't get into trouble. Jonas thought that, well, maybe you would keep an eye on Valiant up here at the library."

There were ten seconds of silence before I responded. "Let me see if I've got this right. The two Vinces and Victor were working on a way to communicate with living selves that involved probably merging with the consciousness of a live person. Am I correct that Valiant was your guinea pig? It didn't go well and Valiant died. Although you don't have a lot of social skills, you were sufficiently aware of the moral implications of what you did to at least take care of the damaged dead self you made. Do I understand this correctly?"

Three of the AtCons were smaller and vibrating faster. The fourth, Valiant, was unchanged. Finally Jonas sent a message to all. "Still bored, Vince? Want to piss her off some more and see what other entertainments she's got up her sleeve?"

Victor sent a message. "Yes, you have it right. Let me proffer a different proposal. Will you join our pod and help us find a way to communicate with the living world?"

"Why? If you wait awhile, everyone you could communicate with will be dead and easily accessible. Why is it so important to communicate with the living now?"

"By our computations based on 2012 statistics, 4,927.7272 children between the ages of one and nineteen years will die in the greater Washington, D.C. metro area. Yet, neither Jonas nor other dead selves we've consulted have ever heard of AtCons in that age range.

"We confirmed that babies less than 1 year old are recycled— their consciousness is merged with a newborn. We monitored hospitals and saw the AtCons migrate from the deceased baby to a baby about to be born. Our theory is that small babies don't have enough memories or knowledge that could overwhelm a newborn infant's development of consciousness. The two either co-exist or merge. However, when babies develop language skills, it is a different matter. We fear that children are being abducted and kept somewhere by dead selves who gain their trust and then merge with them. My son is fourteen and dying of cancer. I don't want to risk him ending up a slave to some pervert."

"Whoa! Slow down. First of all, Victor, I am so sorry that your son is sick. I can't imagine what you are going through. Second, that's a lot of unexpected information to process. None of which answers my question—why is it important to be able to communicate with living people? Take me to the next step."

"Why do we have to answer her questions when the kid could die at any minute." The message came from Vince Senior.

I sensed Victor's efforts to telepath. "Vince Junior has a living friend who is working on research that would permit uploading a living person's memory to a computer until such time as the person can be cloned and the memories downloaded to a new body. If we can communicate with her, my son's memories can be uploaded before he dies. He is not at risk of being tortured by a dead self."

"One thing about being a hillbilly—I can spot bullshit real easy. How many different ways can you insult me? First, you assume that because I'm a woman, I'm the default babysitter. Second, if your concern was what will happen to your son, then you would be hanging out at the hospital where he is and be there to take over his orientation to the afterlife and his protection. How hard is that to figure out?

"Third, I am just speculating here, but because Vince Senior was robbed of his due glory, he wants to have a role in some new wild-assed computer breakthrough and is using your concern for your son to finesse some scheme designed more to aid his agenda than anyone else's. Or else he wouldn't be so edgy right now. You may be brilliant in your fields, but you haven't got the common sense God gave a goose. Must be all that rhetoric about failing fast to learn fast that I got from all my IT contractors at the Defense Department. Well learn this. Fiona Campbell is no fool. I am not helping you communicate with the living because I don't trust you. Particularly you, Vince Senior. But I am babysitting Valiant, the only one of you that I care a flying fuck about. Valiant now hangs with me, for his own good and maybe mine. Anyone here have any problems with that? I am counting to ten to give you time to make your move . . .

"Ten. I am getting no messages, so get lost!"

Jonas appears in a hologram. "Vince old buddy, you just never learn do you? Time to take your Four V's minus one off to where you can lick your wounds." With that, three of the AtCons disappeared.

"Is what they said about children true, Jonas?"

"Yes. I kept a close eye on all dead children, looking for my own. I patrolled a thirty-mile area just in case one of them came back. Slavery is hard on young ones, but nothing. No black, white, any color children have come this way since I died."

"It's not likely that even the most efficient and sinister dead selves could account for all of them. So, where are they?"

"I don't know, but you're probably right. To capture all the dead children would require a kind of organization and infrastructure that just doesn't exist. We can't even communicate with more than a few people at a time and not at all over any distance."

"So, why did you set this up? Why put me through this and risk my being drawn into a sleazy operation like this?"

"I have a certain reputation around here. It's always good to have a favor owed and you were looking for something to do. Quel est le problème, Fiona?

"So this is about your ego. A promise between bros is as good as a bond. Well I won't get in the way of a man and his bros. Take off, hotshot. I need this space to get acquainted with my new friend, Valiant. And note that I have changed your telepath protocol from friend to acquaintance." Jonas disappeared.

"Valiant, did you follow what was going on between your friends and me just now?"

"Yes. You spoke and they heard."

"Hmm. I did get a little excited I guess. I have a hair-trigger temper around sexist men. I want to know that it is okay for you to hang out with me for awhile, just until you get comfortable on your own."

"Sure. I like women better than men to be with. I'm usually a woman."

"What do you mean that you are 'usually' a woman?"

"I am not sure which sex I am. Before I died, I was called "transgendered", because I had male genitalia but liked being a girl. But girl geeks usually dress like the guys, so I was never sure what the difference was. But when I felt sexy, I wanted to touch boys, so maybe I was just gay."

"So, how old were you when you died?"

"Nineteen years, four months, twenty-eight days, fifteen hours, and forty-nine minutes."

"What did your parents think about your gender confusion?"

"I did not know my parents. My grandmother raised me and was pretty confused about everything in the last four years, six months, fourteen days, twenty-three hours and thirteen minutes before I died. I took care of her in our flat in London. I cashed her state pension check, paid the rent, and fetched what we needed from the store around the corner. I spent all my time at home on my computer where I could watch her."

"Not much of a life for either of you. Are you worried about your grandmother?"

Valiant's AtCon became smaller, as if in retreat. "I do not like to think about that. She is fairly helpless without me."

"Would you like to go check on her?"

Valiant's AtCon gets larger and is vibrating in a pink color. "Can we do that? I would like to know that someone found her and took her to a nice place where she can be safe."

"Well that would require a specific address for me to go with you, but you could go just by visualizing your apartment."

"I am afraid to go alone."

"I understand. Let's try this. Do you remember what the front of the library looked like?"

"Sure."

"Then visualize it and you will be there. Once there, visualize this room and you will be back here. Try it by yourself. If anything goes wrong, you can hover in the front door and up the stairs to the third floor."

Valiant's AtCon vibrated even faster, turned a darker rose, then disappeared. Forty seconds later, he reappeared.

"Good job, Valiant! You have mastered teleporting to places you can visualize. This means that you can go to any place in your memory store all by yourself. Jonas told me that if you want to go to places not in your memory store, you have to look up their coordinates on a map or have an address."

"How does all that work? I could telepath when I was alive, but teleporting is really new to me."

"Dang, Valiant! You're full of surprises. What do you mean you could telepath as a live person?"

"I could hear people's thoughts. It's one of the reasons that I stayed inside our flat and lived on a computer. All those other people's thoughts were mostly mean or angry. The terrible things that they wanted to do gutted me. It was better in our dodgy neighborhood to stay inside. So my mates were online. They didn't seem happy either but no one could read anyone's thoughts. I must confess that I can hear your thoughts when you do not intend to send a telepath to me. I hope you are not angry. I mean no rudeness, eavesdropping on your conversations with Jonas just now." His AtCon grew smaller again, its color changing to a pale blue.

"Look, Valiant, I get it. You can't help it so I just ask you to not share any of my thoughts with anyone else. Can you do that?"

"Certainly, Fiona. I can do that. And I can show you how to send songs you sing by telepathy."

"What? First, go check on your grandmother. I will remain here until 7:00 a.m. (EST). If I'm not here when you return, just hang around and wait on me.

Valiant disappeared.

I spent my time waiting for him by finishing Stephen Hawking's A Brief History of Time and perusing The Dancing Wu Li Masters, an older new age treatment of an overview of Newtonian physics and the "new" physics. I dozed off several times slogging through a subject that, even when written so dummies could get it, required my total attention. Although I grasped only the basic rudimentary concepts, I understood that we dead selves functioned under the rules for particle physics. The afterlife was just the natural world navigated in a bodiless atomic configuration of a dead person's consciousness. I REALLY wanted to Google these subjects. Had the three Vs known me at all, they would have offered me a way to connect to the Internet, not living people. I still don't get what that's all about.

My pessimism was set aside when Valiant returned full of jubilant excitement. "I found her. I found her in our old apartment." Valiant was vibrating a nice soft coral tone.

"Was she all right?"

"Yes, she was dead, but that is a big improvement for Grandmother. Her AtCon had shrunk to the size of a pea and was caught in a cobweb in our living room's light fixture. She was pretty knackered. Other people were living there and I guess she took refuge in the light fixture. We talked and once she was feeling more secure, I helped her get to her church to stay. She is far more chipper there and is reviewing her happy memories and some of her favorite soap operas. I am not sure she can tell the difference, actually. But that is permissible, is it not?"

"As far as I know, Valiant, dead selves don't have to be smart. You did well. Are you back to stay?"

"I am full of doubt. I need to learn more about being dead since I would like to see the world and have meaningful relationships. Those are relationships full of meaning. Logic dictates that another woman like you could help me with that.

"Fiona, do you think that as a dead self where no one can really tell what I look like that I might find someone to love me? When you look at my AtCon, what do you see? Do I look like a girl? I notice that I give off a pink color."

"All anyone can see is a soft light that seems to change based on your mood. Sometimes the light has elliptical lines that vibrate when dead selves are emotional—like angry or feeling sad. I don't think pink means the dead self is a female. Jonas sometimes has a pink or reddish color.

"Valiant, you are one of the most loveable people I know— dead or alive. In time, you will find someone to love you in a special way that goes with feeling sexy. It is important to prepare yourself to be a good partner when the time comes."

"What makes someone a good partner, Fiona?"

"I honestly don't know, Valiant." Memories of being dumped by boyfriends flashed through my brain. Scenes where I was angry and they were crying or they were angry and I was angrier. And a lot of guilt. Why was guilt such a big part of my memory of failed relationships?

Valiant noticed my change in mood. "You are feeling sad now. You want to cry. No one will want me if I make them cry!"

"Shhh. You didn't cause my sadness. Your question was a good one. I was sad because I couldn't answer it. I didn't have much luck with men when I was alive, and I tried many times."

"Maybe, Fiona, you should try with women then."

"You made me laugh! You might have something there, Valiant. But first, I'm going home to West Virginia. See if I can find my mother and father. They have been dead for some time, but maybe their AtCons can be found near the little town where they lived when they died. My feelings about them are very confusing and my memories. . .I can't bring myself to look at them."

"Before I go, I am projecting a scan of two books about physics for you to copy. While I'm gone, read these and see what you can make of them. You should be safe here in the library for a day or two. Is that okay with you?"

"Sure. I like it here. There are hardly any people in the library. I like being on my own. I will strive to be an effective adult while you are gone. If I get bored, I will remember all the chocolate I ate in my life."

CHAPTER 4

I teleported to the Glover Gap Cemetery in Marion County, West Virginia. The cemetery overlooked a creek framed by willow trees at the bottom of the hill. Families of the dead kept the banks mowed when they mowed the cemetery, so it became a playground of sorts for kids. It would be deserted on a school day and thus a good place for me to prepare myself. I wasn't sure that I could make contact with either parent or what I would do if I did. I just knew that so far in my existence as a dead self, I was repeating all my live self bad habits. I didn't have to come down on the geeks like I did. Why did I like to power up around men? No wonder men ran from me. I really was a castrating bitch a lot of times. Then I feel guilty for hurting their feelings. Fuck, what am I doing here? Well, I'm here, so I will give it a go starting with my mother.

My earliest memories were of my mother's face with brown hair pulled close to her head, large brown eyes, and a small mole on her pale cheek. She smelled like almonds from the Jergens hand lotion that she favored. She was warm and hummed tuneless songs that made her chest vibrate against my head when she rocked me.

I jumped ahead to when my baby brother died, when everything changed. I was four years, one month, eighteen days, and twenty-two hours old. I didn't know Todd very long, but I knew he was in my family. Before he died, when I pretended that my Cheerios were people and I was a giant eating them up, I would leave three Cheerios floating in the milk—one for Daddy, one for Momma, and one for Todd. After Todd died, I only left two Cheerios.

I also recalled Momma being sad and crying a lot. Daddy seldom came home and when he did, he was mean to Momma. They argued and once a doctor came to the house to take care of Momma 'cause she was screaming real loud. Daddy took me to the neighbors for several nights and I played with the Jenkins boys and ate honey spooned on buttered biscuits.

Things quieted down after awhile and I started school. My memories were less of my parents and more of school and playmates except on holidays. Daddy was like a kid during holidays, especially Christmas. Every Christmas memory after age six was a version of the first one. Daddy would take me out with him to cut down a tree, one that I picked out. He would make much of the tree's special qualities as he carried it over his shoulder and we would sing all the Christmas songs I knew on the cold walk home. He and I decorated the tree while Momma just looked on and kept busy cleaning and waxing or sewing on her treadle sewing machine.

Then something happened and Momma disappeared into the spare bedroom and I had to be quiet and not bother her. Grown-ups stopped talking when I came into the room. My aunt and uncle came to take me to live with them on their farm for a while. It was the best summer of my life. My Aunt Hattie baked cookies with me, taught me to play Chinese checkers, and tucked me in at night. I had other children to play with and there was never a lonely moment.

When I went home again, Momma was gone. When I asked where she was, Daddy said he didn't know. First time I repeated the question, he slapped me. Soon afterwards, he bought a television set for us to watch. No one in Glover Gap had a television back then so I was very proud and had friends over to watch Howdy Doody. I still missed Momma, but I liked being Daddy's special girl—taking care of the house and helping him cook dinner. Most of all, I liked cuddling with Daddy on the couch watching television. Now that I'm dead, I can fill in all the blanks in my childhood memories after that. How the cuddling slowly became something else. How old was I when the line was crossed? When did I become culpable?

At age eleven, children were readied by the Baptist church to take Jesus as their Savior. I won the silver dollar my year for being able to recite all the books in the Bible better than anyone else in my Sunday school class. I felt very grown up and serious when I was dunked in the creek and baptized that summer day. But I knew something was wrong. I wasn't like the other children in the line with me. I was pretty sure that they did not do the things I did with my daddy with the lights out watching the television. I knew it was wrong even if I did not have the words to describe the wrongness. Daddy made me promise that I would never tell anyone. But I never saw anyone on television doing those things.

I cried myself to sleep, full of a nameless shame and anxiety. I knew God could see what I did and I would be punished. I spent the summer I turned twelve with my aunt and uncle again as had become the custom and pushed my shame into a compartment that I pretended did not exist. I made up stories about good wholesome things that Daddy and I did at home and tried to believe my made-up home life.

At summer's end, the excitement of riding on the big yellow school bus to the junior high school in Mannington gave me a new life. I walked the half mile to my grandmother's house after school where I helped her with dinner. When Daddy got off from work, we would eat supper there. On Saturdays, I cleaned our house all day and did the wash. Sunday was church and Sunday school. I stopped watching television then, claiming I had homework to do. I avoided my father and he did not press me. I wanted to be like the other girls and I wanted God's forgiveness.

The following year, I was in eighth grade and had friends and belonged to a school club. I also got my period and breasts. Boys noticed me. Since unsupervised dating before age seventeen was generally frowned upon, the Mannington Volunteer Fire Department held socials in the school gym—sock hops—to raise money and provide a safe place where teens too young to date could socialize. I loved to dance to the music and flirt with boys and swirl my skirts; but my daddy didn't approve. He became adamant that I was too young. Even my grandmother could not change his mind. I took it as God's punishment that I not join in with the good Christian kids. I was so filled with guilt that I accepted my father's will as just. I worked hard at school, prayed for forgiveness and counted the days till summer and I could be with my aunt and uncle where I felt normal.

Things between my father and me changed when I was fifteen and finishing ninth grade. I won a typing contest sponsored by the coal company, the biggest employer in Mannington. My prize was a summer job as a work-study student in their offices. My grandmother made sure that I had enough skirts and blouses to mix and match for a five-day workweek. I stayed with her and my single aunts who loaned me jewelry and fixed my hair so I would look "businesslike". Every payday, I deposited my check in my new savings account at the Mannington State Bank, reviewing the stamped entries on my passbook with pride. I spent that money over and over again in my head.

A week before the start of my sophomore year, the job ended and I had to return home. I threw myself into cleaning and cooking, trying to catch up with piles of dirty laundry. I was hanging clothes on the line when Daddy called me from the kitchen. "Fiona, bring me a small flat-head screwdriver with a long shank."

He was down on the floor working under the sink in the kitchen. When I kneeled down and held out the screwdriver. He grabbed me, pulling me on top of him and, pushing his tongue into my mouth. I swung the screwdriver clutched in my fist into his side. He flinched in pain as I scrambled away from him, wiping my mouth, spitting on him and shaking with fear and revulsion.

I ran through the woods to the cemetery where children were playing in the creek. Under the weeping willow, partially hidden and all but ignored by the kids splashing in the water. I hid all that long hot August night, long after everyone was gone. When I was sure that my Daddy had left for work the next morning, I finished the laundry, packed my clothes in some cardboard boxes, and pushed them in the wheelbarrow up the road to the highway. I waited by the mailboxes until a car came along that I knew and I waved it down. My neighbor took me and my boxes of 'donations for the church collection' to Grandmother's house. I told her that Daddy and I had a terrible fight and I would not go back. She rolled her eyes like I was being contrary and would come to my senses once I cooled off.

I watched the playback of the rest of that afternoon, a turning point in my life. I saw myself walk to the mine office in my shabby shirt and jeans where I waited outside until closing when my boss would come out and be alone.

"You said you liked my work, Mr. Coleman, so I was wondering if I could keep on after school this year. I could catch up on the back filing and since I'm taking shorthand, I could also take dictation. I'd be part-time, so you wouldn't have to pay me as much."

"Fiona, honey, we don't have any openings or really need more help. But wait a minute; I saw a notice on the bulletin board about someone needing a babysitter. Let's go take a look at that. Yeah, here it is." He pulled the tacked note off and handed it to me. "Call that number and tell them that I sent you. Come next summer, it'll be a different story. I don't forget a good worker."

He walked me to the door and held it while I stared at the scrap of pink paper, my head down to hide tears welling in my eyes. "Thanks, Mr. Coleman. I'll call tonight."

I had no plan to check on the babysitting job—those jobs typically pay enough for a movie ticket—but I had no other place to go and the address wasn't much out of my way to my grandmother's. As I approached the little brick house, I could hear kids yelling and a woman's tired voice. A small bike was lying across the sidewalk and a red ball was resting in a rhododendron bush. The door was standing ajar so I stuck my head in and hollered, "Hello. Mrs. Marchat!"

The door suddenly swung open with the help of a lanky boy whose head came up to my shoulder. "Momma, some lady is here." He then jumped on top of a smaller, tow-head boy on the sofa and started pounding him with a boxing glove with "Pow! Pow! Pow!" sound effects.

Jennifer Marchat peered around the corner. I don't think I have ever seen as angelic a face as hers. Thick, light blond hair, falling in waves and curls to her shoulders like an ornate, gilt frame for a smooth cameo face. I stammered as best I could, "I came about the babysitting job." I held out the hand clutching the crumpled slip of paper.

"Come on in. I'm in the middle of cleaning up a dirty butt. You might as well see what the job entails first hand." She disappeared around the corner, leaving me to catch up with her as she walked quickly to the third door at the end of the hall. There I found baby Eliza in her crib, naked as a jaybird, chubby hands waving in the air.

The room was filled with the smell of baby poop, but Eliza was about to pass Jennifer's clean-butt inspection. Bending over the baby, Jennifer deftly lifted Eliza over the folded diaper and fastened the thick folds of cloth with safety pins. "Now for a clean top." Jennifer sat Eliza up and slipped a cotton shirt over her plump belly. "And a whoop-dee-do leap in the air." Jennifer lifted Eliza high in the air then brought her down for a snuggle. "I am going to miss this," she said to no one in particular.

"Here, you take her and I'll wash my hands and meet you in the living room. Boys! Go outside or go to bed! I cannot stand you another minute!" Jennifer once again left me on my own and I stared at Eliza's plump, happy face.

I shifted the strange weight of the baby around until I felt confident that I could walk and not drop her. She leaned back from me and her face contorted into a scowl that would surely lead to a scream. I smiled and jiggled her up and down. It was the only mothering move I had at the time. As we entered the living room, she noticed the boys now outside making boy noise. She perked up and waved her arms at them and smiled. I stood at the door and waited for Jennifer, afraid to break Eliza's eye contact with her brothers.

The house's clutter and noise reminded me of my aunt and uncle's place. Jennifer invited me to sit but did not offer to take Eliza. I sat down on the sofa, which caused Eliza to lose sight of the boys and recall that a stranger held her. She started snuffling. I smiled and cooed. I jiggled frantically. I was about to lose this job. I sat her on my lap facing me. "Well Miss Eliza. What seems to be the matter? Did you lose your toes? Well, here they are!" I tickled the sole of her foot. She pulled it back but laughed. I knew I had her then. "Or did you lose your belly button?" I tipped her back and blew loudly on her belly. "There it is." Now she was cackling.

"Yes, I'm going to miss all of this," said Jennifer wistfully. "Well, I think you are cute as a bug and Eliza sure likes you, but I need someone who can work all shifts. I'm a nurse at the hospital in Fairmont. You look like you're still in high school."

"Mr. Coleman told me to tell you that he sent me. I'm a good worker." I replied like English wasn't my mother tongue. I shook my head hard and stared at Eliza's belly button. "I can certainly be here for two of your shifts, and the boys look like they are school age, so there would just be the baby. If you could find someone to keep the baby until I'm home from school, it would work."

The silence that followed begged to be filled.

"I'll work for my room and board. It would cost you nothing." By now, my tears were splashing on Eliza's tummy and it was totally obvious that I was just a scared kid. Desperation eating my insides, I blurted, "I can do your housework and washing too."

I saw Jennifer's hands taking the baby from me. What woman would leave her children with a sniveling fifteen-year-old? I dabbed my eyes with the hem of my skirt. "I'm sorry to act a fool. It's kind a been a bad day and I'm tired."

She sat down beside me and moved Eliza to her lap. Then she put her arm around me. I lowered my head to rest on her shoulder. "Thank you," I whispered.

Eliza patted my face and grinned. I had to laugh and then I cried some more and we three hugged and rocked to and fro for a few minutes. Jennifer jumped up and said, "What's your name, darlin'?"

"Fiona Campbell, from Glover Gap."

"Well, come on in the kitchen and hold this young'un while I fix us some supper. You'll stay won't you? I'm making my famous tuna casserole and I have corn on the cob and sliced tomatoes."

I held the baby while Jennifer washed her hands again, then it was my turn to wash my hands while Eliza sat in her high chair eating Cheerios. About midway into getting supper ready, Jennifer asked, "how do you know Sam Coleman?"

I told her about my summer job and answered some questions about myself. I knew she would want to know why I was willing to work for my keep, so I just brazenly told her. Not the truth, but enough of the truth. "I can't live with my father. It's just too hard and my grandmother doesn't see my side. He's her son and he helps her out from time to time. I don't want to put her in the middle."

"Fiona, am I going to have trouble with your father if I take you in?" she asked, her eyes boring into mine.

"Maybe. Probably. I don't know." I dropped my head and kept slicing tomatoes.

"Where would you go if I didn't take you in?" she asked.

"Pittsburgh. I have all my paychecks from this summer in the bank. I would run away to Pittsburgh." Until I heard the words coming out of my mouth, I was unaware I'd ever given any thought to Pittsburgh.

"Well then, you can stay here as long as you need to. You can earn your keep cleaning and doing laundry and keeping an eye on the boys when they're home from school. I'll leave the baby with Mrs. Fenester next door. The deal is off if you break any of my million rules. You must learn first aid, which I will teach you, and never take your eyes off the boys. If you can handle all that, we have a deal."

Jennifer met daddy late one night a week later in the Emergency Room when he staggered in feverish, drooling, and unable to talk. Following medical protocol at the time, she relieved his pain from the tetanus infection. Eventually, a doctor arrived who pronounced him dead. If Jennifer made any connection between his infected puncture wound and my leaving home, she never mentioned it. He was a miner. Accidents happened all the time.

I had one year of high school as a normal girl—no shame, no guilt, no overbearing father, but lots of work. If Jennifer hadn't married Sam Coleman the next summer and moved to Charleston, I would have stayed longer. But by that time, I had a letter of recommendation from Mr. Coleman attesting to my secretarial skills, ten years of public schooling, a driver's license that said I was 18, and Jennifer as an inspiration for my future. She had gone to college to be a nurse and convinced me that I could do the same.

As I look back on those days, my first meeting with Jennifer was both my happiest and saddest memory and left me fervently believing in guardian angels for a time. She was sent by God to save me. She was a sign. He forgave me. I could search every memory and not find another time when I got a break like that one. I still have the pink slip of paper pressed in my old Bible.

If I have learned anything in the years since, it is that only time can tell the difference between good luck and bad because most times they are just different sides of the same event. With her loving, courageous heart, Jennifer saved me from a horrible threat that fate would have eliminated a few days hence anyhow. But by doing so, she set me up to be abandoned a third time when she yielded to her new husband's wishes to leave me behind.

I was ready to meet my parents if they were here. There was no longer anything to fear or dread. They were in my past. I concentrated on Momma first. I didn't know where she would go in reaction to the death fright, but was sure it wouldn't be our old house. The Glover Gap graveyard was as good a place as any to send a message.

"Amanda Glover Campbell. Your daughter Fiona Campbell asks to speak and be heard." I repeated the message with my full volume. I waited for two minutes and repeated the telepath again. And again for an hour. By then, schoolchildren were showing up on their way home. So I teleported to Grandmother's house.

The house seemed empty. It had not been painted in some time and a few windows had broken panes. Filled with dread despite my resolve, I toured each familiar room. No furniture or personal belongings remained inside, so I telepathed to my father. "Robert Mitchell Campbell, your daughter Fiona Campbell asks to speak and be heard." I waited. In the middle of my second attempt, I felt a strong draft whirling around from all directions at once.

I could see a blue-gray light of an AtCon in the direction of the kitchen. "Is that you, Father?" I could not bring myself to call him "Daddy".

"Yes. So you are dead now."

"Obviously."

"I've been waiting to settle scores with you for a long time, Fiona."

"Well, old man, I was just too busy living my life to give much thought to your wishes. But now that I'm dead, I have plenty of time. One might say, that I can work on your suffering for all eternity. How does that thought strike you?"

"You ungrateful child! If it weren't for me taking care of you, you'd've starved and died alone in that shack in Glover Gap. After your mother left, I was all you had and you were all I had and we could have been happy if some young stud at Mannington High School hadn't caught your eye."

"Do you think that I left home so I could be with some boy at school? Find me something in your memory store that suggested a boy in my life."

"You kept wanting to go to those dances to wiggle your ass to music. I watched you. I saw how they looked at you. But it was me that fed you, gave you a home and I deserved to be the first with you, not them. But your daddy wasn't good enough."

Four minutes passed in silence.

"Let me see if I got this right. You used a daughter who adored you for sex. You sacrificed the childhood of a little girl to indulge your lust. You made me complicit in your offense. You are a stupid, impotent excuse of a man who preyed on those weaker than him, too lazy or cheap to find a whore. And your defense is that feeding me for fifteen years gave you dibs on my virginity. Is that your complaint with me, you ravenous beast in the field? I'm not sufficiently beholden for the food you provided? I'm glad that I killed you, you sorry sonofabitch. If only I could kill you again.

"Say your final say, you disgusting piece of shit. I am done with you! You are not my father and the family that spawned you is not my family. My children and their children will never know of you. Your line is ended and I bar you from all contact with me."

"Proud words they are, little girl. But in your memory store are the good days when your father took you to find Christmas trees, and made you believe about Santa Claus cause he made sure you had gifts under that tree. Times when we loved each other. You will never be free of me. Those memories bind us no matter what followed after. It's the good memories that will do you in, not the bad ones."

The light of his AtCon faded and he was gone. He'd had the last word, and he was right. I can easily avoid the bad memories. It's the good ones that make me hurt for what I lost.

The confrontation brought me no relief. Now that I know why I am angry, I'm still angry. And defeated. I was ready to go back to Maryland. I hovered around over Glover Gap to see what it looks like from the air. It took several tries before I was able to hover over the cemetery. As I wobbled through the air, recording the view for later, I heard a tuneless humming in the distance. I telepathed my coordinates in Maryland, just in case.

NOW THAT I'M DEAD

CHAPTER 5

Valiant was in the library, reading. "Hey pal. What have I missed?

"Fiona! I am so glad you are back, mate. I feared for you after what Mr. Jonas said."

"What did he say?"

"That you were crazy for going off on your own. Then he started listing all the things that could happen to you—swallowed by a large bird, accidentally merged with a rabbit or squirrel, electrically charged by running into a power line or being struck by lightning, abducted by irate misogynists, shoved under a rock by Christians, or getting lost and never finding your way back."

"Did you tell him where I'd gone?"

"No, you told me I should keep what you say to me confidential. So I just said that you went away and I could not tell him where. He seemed to think that meant that I did not know where you went, which struck me as strange since that is not what I said. I heard him think that he was a fool for pissing you off and he wondered why you were mad at him for trying to get you to look after me when that is what you did anyhow. He thinks you are a pain in the ass."

"Valiant, who else knows that you can read minds?" I sent the message cloaked as confidential.

"Only you among the dead selves," he messaged.

"Let's keep it that way for now until we know who can be trusted."

"Fiona, why WERE you so mad at the Geeks Anonymous for doing what they did to get you to look after me when you really did not mind looking after me?"

"It's no big mystery that people don't like being manipulated, especially through lies. I was angry over that, not that they wanted me to look after you. They should have used the magic words."

"Abracadabra?"

"No. 'Please' and 'thank you' are the magic words. Asking shows respect while tricking someone shows disrespect. All they had to do was ask me if I would please take care of you while they worked on their radio signals. Besides, lies make me angry. Don't tell lies, Valiant." I knew the minute that the words were out of my mouth that I would regret them. Valiant would now be unable to tell even the whitest lie. Time to change the subject. "How much did you read while I was gone?"

Valiant's AtCon turned bright pink and started vibrating. "All of it. It was blindingly brilliant! It explains a lot of the weird things I saw when I was recording the circuits of the hard drives of computers for Geeks Anonymous. I had to get very small to get into the chips and see how they worked and when I did, I saw little tunnels throughout this thick soup of suspended particles. I was afraid I would fall into one. Now I think they could be tunnels to other times or even other universes. Is that possible? I wish I knew a real physicist to ask, but all the famous ones in the books are dead except for Stephen Hawking."

"Valiant! You are brilliant! Yes, they are dead, just like us. We can talk to them if we can find them. See if you can find out where they lived when they died. Damn. If only we could Google their names! There must be some way to get online. Think, Valiant. Think! Now I know why Jonas started falling behind other students once they got PCs."

"Did someone call my name?" Jonas' hologram appears from behind a stack of books.

40

"Are you now reduced to eavesdropping?" Why did I say that?

"I hesitate to remind you that this is a public library, a place that had been my residence long before I invited you here. Sometimes you are as gracious as a spoiled child!"

Before I could extricate my foot from my mouth, I was stopped by Jonas' use of the words "spoiled child." My father's rant echoed in my head and a feeling of revulsion shot through me. I had to get away! My AtCon shrunk and the next thing I knew, I was in the magnolia tree. Jonas was soon by my side.

"Fiona, I'm so sorry for blowing off like I do, which usually gets us bantering back and forth, but I hurt you somehow. I didn't mean to. Sweet girl, tell me what is wrong? Where were you all day?"

"I'm tired. How come dead selves get tired? Is it the teleporting?" My telepath was weak.

"Rest here tonight. I'll stay with you." His AtCon moved close to mine, suspended an inch or two above a patch of leaves. I felt myself drifting into the oblivion of sleep.

"Can you hear the owl?" Jonas sent the message to a drowsy woman. "There has always been an owl around here. It must live in the old barn. Soon there'll be lightning bugs to watch. They come right up in the trees to mate. This time of year is nice in Maryland. Sleep now.

"Israel, my love. I miss you."

* * *

A beam of sunlight found its way through the upper branches to where I was suspended in space, waking me to a bright early summer morning. I had slept seven hours, twenty-three minutes, and forty-eight seconds. My AtCon expanded a bit as I went to the top of the tree to check things out. Maryland is nice this time of year. Did I hear an owl last night? I could remember little after Jonas arrived and said he would stay with me. I do feel safer with Jonas around. Where is he?

"Looking for me?" Jonas asked from the other side of the walnut grove. Then he was beside me. "Feeling better?"

"Yes, I actually feel pretty good. Don't know what came over me last night. I knew you were teasing. Thanks for keeping an eye out for me last night, but we should get back to Valiant and compare notes on how we can get our AtCons to be more useful. Race you . . . ." Damn! He's gone.

It is a weekend and the microfiche archives are empty except for three AtCons. I spy Valiant up near a window. He seems suspended in space, maybe asleep. I whisper, "Hey, Valiant. Rise and shine!"

"No. No. Not now. I am making a scrummy dream with both chocolate and a meaningful relationship in it."

"Sorry, bud, we three need to put our AtCons together and see what we know from our research on particle physics and our AtCons."

Valiant's AtCon grew and bobbed a few times. How does he do that? It's like a cat stretching.

Jonas led the discussion while Valiant listened politely, his AtCon bobbing nervously. After waffling around comparing basic Newtonian and particle physics, Jonas wrapped up by telling us what we already knew about the AtCon and how they made life pretty comfortable for dead selves. It was pretty lame for someone who has had two lifetimes using an AtCon. Jonas had to know more than he was sharing. Once his commercial message concluded, I passed the baton to Valiant.

"Valiant, what got you so excited yesterday?" I was proving myself deserving of Jonas's ungrateful child tribute. Sweet words don't buy much from Fiona Campbell.

"Oh, yes. That. I think I know how we teleport. When we teleport, we instantly reduce our size so small that we can enter one of the other ten dimensions to take a shortcut across the flattened one-time, three-dimensional space scenario that is how the Newtonian world appears. That's because space-time is on a curve and in the world of subatomic particles, there are all these small curves representing many more dimensions that are only large enough for a tiny subatomic particle to enter. We can just enter one of those and take short cuts to other points in the Newtonian world. I still don't know how we find the right path to where we want to be, but as far as I know, it always works. Maybe our AtCons are all part of everything else and know where everything is and how to get us there but it is automatic like keeping proper time."

42

"Autonomic is the term, Valiant." Jonas added.

"Or is it?" I interjected. "Why do we automatically report time with so much precision? That's not anything we learned as live selves, but as dead selves, we seem to have no choice. Same thing with using the metric system. They may properly be thought of as autonomic, but why? Why can't dead selves leave off the time zone data. And why do we have to report hours when we start with a year and seconds when we start with less than a year?"

Jonas responded, "Let Valiant finish and we can come back to that."

"Thank you, Jonas. The most important thing I figured out is this. From now on, I want to be called Valerie, not Valiant. I prefer to be a female, like Fiona. And I want to say 'Fuck' whenever I want."

Who knew Valiant was this smart? How do I protect him, er, her from the geeks if they get wind of this? And no one knows she can read minds as well.

"Well, I think you have earned those privileges," Jonas said. "What do you say, Fiona? Can you spare some salty language for Valerie here?"

"Sure. Welcome to the world of uppity women, Valerie. I will help you make that transition. Count on it, sweetpea."

"But given your genius around all things related to our AtCons, I'm more concerned that no one takes advantage of you. So, can we agree to keep this information to ourselves for now? What do you say, Jonas?"

"Yeah. I say we do more than keep it quiet. Let's form a pod for mutual protection."

Having Valerie close enough to read Jonas' mind might clear up some of the mysteries around Jonas. I moved closer to Valerie. "Yes to the pod idea. What about you, Valerie? Want to be part of our pod?"

"I did not like being part of the Geeks Anonymous pod. I know that I like being with Fiona because she cares about me. Do you care about me, Jonas? Are you someone I can trust?"

"Not sure how to answer your question, but I will make you and Fiona a promise. I will never knowingly do anything to hurt either of you. I will keep the secrets of the pod and I will warn you if I am aware of any danger to you. And I will consider your request for other concessions that may come up later, like not going behind your back to trick you into doing something. Does that return me to your good graces, Fiona?"

I sent a cloaked message to Valerie. "Is he telling the truth?" "Yes" was her reply.

"I'm good if Valerie is," I announced.

"We are a pod!!" Valerie broadcast. "What will our pod name be? Will the library be our home? Is Jonas like a father now? And Fiona is like a mother?"

Jonas seemed awfully pleased with himself. What had I missed? Oh yes, we are no longer on the topic of AtCons. I hope my gamble of keeping him close to Valerie and Valerie close to me does not backfire. At some point, Jonas has to learn that his thoughts are open to Valerie and that we've deceived him about that. That will be an awkward conversation. I'm tricking him; a violation of the pod agreement that I just made seconds ago. I need a moment to think about what I'm doing.

"I'm going to let you two get to know each other better, while I'm making a visit to Potomac Gardens. It just dawned on me that one of my fellow inmates was a physicist."

I teleported to Potomac Gardens, eager to see Bennet Soren again. Now there was a man I could trust. So gentle and kind. Bennet was a long-time divorcée with two children, Mark and Kate. Mark was a doctor out west somewhere; Kate was single and worked on Capitol Hill. Samantha, Mark's daughter, was the apple of Bennet's eye and they Skyped every week. I found Bennet in his suite asleep. It was only 6:00 p.m. (EST), so I wondered about that. I looked through some papers on his desk. One was a letter from his attorney saying that the recent changes in his will were made to exclude Mark and Mark's wife Amelia as heirs, leaving his entire estate shared equally between Kate and Samantha. How odd that he would cut Mark and Amelia out of his will. They must be dead! That has to be the reason. Shit. Bennet must be devastated.

I called up my memories of our conversations about our respective medical issues. Bennet had emphysema and took a statin drug. We gloated that neither of us was diabetic. In places like Potomac Gardens, residents who had regular bowel movements were entitled to bragging rights, but to hit seventy-five and be diabetes-free was the equivalent of being crowned prom king or queen. If we had only known that at the end of our lives a healthy digestive track and ability to recognize family members would assure us the envy of our peers, then we might have taken the cruel rejections of our adolescence with more grace.

I hung out in his room until things quieted down and Gina, the supervisor, would be watching TV in the main recreation parlor. Once in her office, I found the "S" file drawer and got my AtCon down small enough to get inside. There, I used my glow to find Bennet Soren's file with handwritten case notes. Potomac Gardens was transitioning from paper to electronic records under the purview of old Dr. Woodson. He was terrified of computers and didn't embrace the change, so for the moment, Potomac Gardens kept redundant files. I saw where Bennet was on antidepressants, not the nibbles of Xanax that they hand out like after-dinner mints, but the heavy-duty stuff—Nardil. No wonder he was asleep.

I kept looking for something from Woodson and finally found it. "Severe depression at death of son and daughter-in-law in car accident. Not responding to psychotherapy. Not eating. Not ambulatory. July 12, 2014." That was two days ago.

I had two conflicting thoughts. Bennet may be joining the dead selves soon and he would be perfect for our pod. But his granddaughter needed him alive. Well, I could not influence how any of this turned out, but if he did die, I wanted to be here.

I stopped by his room again. This time I saw a soft blue glow the size of a quarter just above the window blinds. I telepathed the message, "This is Bennet's friend, Fiona. I invite you to be an acquaintance. Speak and be heard." There was no response, but the AtCon shrank. "Don't be afraid. I can't hurt you. Do you know Bennet?"

"Father," was weakly telepathed.

I tried again. "Are you Mark?"

"Yes. Who are you?"

"I'm Fiona, formerly a resident here and a friend of your father's. How long have you been dead, Mark?"

"Two weeks, three days, six hours, twenty-three minutes, and nineteen seconds. Are you dead as well?"

"If we can communicate, we are both dead. Is Amelia with you?"

"No, she is watching Samantha. She can't bear to be away from her."

"Is Samantha okay?"

"Yes. She was not with us when we died. How do you know my father?"

"One month, three weeks, three days, four hours, and twenty-three seconds ago, I lived in Suite 106. Poor Bennet, he lost a son and Amelia whom he loved like a daughter. How is Samantha handling this?"

"Not well. She is only twelve and this is a lot for her to deal with. Kate is with her at our place, where they will stay until Sam is ready to come back with Kate. It is good to have someone dead to talk to. I am learning my way around by trial and error."

"It helps to have someone show you the ropes. I can stay for a while if there is anything I can do. Are you worried about Bennet?"

"Yes. I came here two days ago. Took me that long to learn how to use coordinates. Sometimes I think I am caught up in a crazy dream. None of this is real. I can't use tools or turn on a light switch, or DO anything. As a doctor, I can make some deductions based on his treatment, but I really need to examine him and read his chart. I'm afraid someone will see me."

"Well, I can help you with that. Living selves can't see your glow, only dead selves. Dead selves can't hurt you unless you give them permission to merge with you, in which case they could mess with your memories. Reviewing happy memories is like a recreation now. Try it to help you relax and adjust to the sudden change in your environment. Another thing, dead selves need to sleep. Are you sleeping?"

"No, I'm afraid Dad will die. I need to watch so I can be here to help him."

"You need to sleep or you will be too weak to help him. Your AtCon holds its position while you sleep, so make yourself comfortable tonight while I watch. Then at 7:00 a.m., you can read over Dr. Woodson's shoulder and do your own examination. Probably a better one since your sensors are more acute. I will show you as much as I can tomorrow morning. Give me time to let my pod back at the University of Maryland library know where I am. You don't have to do this all by yourself."

"You would do that?"

"It's not like I have a heavy schedule these days, Mark. Back in a flash."

NOW THAT I'M DEAD

CHAPTER 6

Mark slept the rest of the night and woke me abruptly at 6:45 a.m. (EST) "What are you doing asleep? You're supposed to be watching!" His telepath whacked me with its intensity.

"Relax, sport. I was watching." Jonas' AtCon increased in size and moved closer to Mark. "Let me introduce myself, I am Jonas and a friend to Fiona. I can assure you that Bennet has been checked several times by nurses and he is still very much alive. Dr. Woodson has had his breakfast and is now in the men's room completing his morning toilet after drinking three cups of coffee."

"How do you feel, Mark?" I asked to change the direction of the conversation.

"Much better. I guess living people can't hear us either."

"That's because we are not making any noise. You are reading my thoughts. It's called 'telepathy.'" Jonas was being obnoxious.

"Mark, I hear the doctor coming. Listen up. You can record written material by just scanning it quickly. Run your eyes over it like you were speed reading and a copy will be retained in your memory that you can review at your leisure." I moved out of the way and sent a telepath to Jonas to join me.

Mark's AtCon became very animated as it hovered just over Woodson's right ear. He read the first page and hesitated. I forgot to tell him about getting small enough to go between pages, so I demonstrated. I scanned the rest and sent him a telepath that I had copied the six pages of material. By that time he was focused on the meds that were left in a paper cup. Then he darted over to hover over the blood pressure gauge.

Dr. Woodson has the supervisor with him. "Gina, let's hook him up to a heart and blood pressure monitor and put him on an IV drip of Myer's solution with Vitamin C. In addition, give him as much of our rehydration beverages that he will drink. His eyes are dilated and not reacting to light. No more Nardil until we get his blood pressure back up. If he does not come around by noon, call me and I will prescribe Adderall to counter the Nardil. If he does wake, get him to eat solid foods and walk some."

The minute the room cleared of the live selves, Mark erupted. "They have him on Nardil. It's one of the first generation antidepressants that no one but that old codger would still be using. Nardil is dangerous when combined with amphetamines and it also acts as a sedative. Nor should he be eating solid food with fluid in his lungs. The last thing we need is his coughing up food into his compromised lungs. Using an amphetamine to rouse him will cause his blood pressure to spike; the minute that shows on the monitor, some nurse will give him either a diuretic or a beta blocker that will cause symptoms of depression and asthma. Where did this man get his medical training? I need to know how much oxygen is in his blood. See if that is in the notes you took, Fiona."

"I don't see any blood test for oxygen. Here, read it for yourself." I telepathed the three pages that I had copied in Gina's office.

"They aren't looking at that at all. I can hear the fluid in both lower lobes of his lungs. Why can't they hear it? Is there some way we can raise his head?"

"None that I know of. Our AtCons can't interact with the natural world. Isn't that right, Jonas?" I looked for his AtCon but couldn't see it. "Where did he go?"

About then, an orderly came in with the monitoring equipment. We waited for the staff to hook up everything so that Mark could monitor his vital signs, but no one appeared. Several hours passed and Bennet remained asleep. Mark's AtCon was vibrating a dark khaki green and moving restlessly around the room.

"How small can I get in this AtCon? Small enough to enter his bloodstream?"

"I don't know. Valerie has mapped circuits in computer motherboards, but she wasn't happy about it. I think when you get that small, the laws of physics change."

"Yes, I know. Nanotechnology has given us great diagnostic tools in medicine. We can send a small camera into almost any body organ, including the blood vessels. If my AtCon could be reduced small enough without hurting me, I could just take a quick tour of Dad's lungs."

"How would you breathe?"

"How do I breathe right now?"

"Good point. Jonas, we need you. Come if you can hear me."

After trying several times at intervals of two minutes, thirty seconds, I had another thought. "Let me go get Valerie."

Valerie was nowhere to be found at the library. I tried telepathing her with no luck either. I returned to Bennet's room thinking how difficult it is to communicate at any distance. I can't even leave a note much less a voice mail. "Sorry Mark. No one is around." Including Mark. I looked closely at Bennet's nose using 4X magnification. It was pretty hairy, but dry, which I knew was not a good thing for a dog. I shrunk to the size of a pea, which is the smallest I have ever been, but if Valerie's grandmother could do it with no ill effects, so could I.

"Hello, Mark!! Are you inside Bennet? Do you need help?"

"I'm stuck in some phlegm in his left bronchial tube. I can't see anything."

"You can generate more light by increasing your vibration. May also free you from the phlegm."

Bennet coughed. He coughed again and out popped a small gob of mucous.

"Well, all I learned is that he is waking up and his bronchial tubes are congested, which I could hear anyhow. What time is it?"

"12:33 p.m. (EST). The doctor was here five hours ago and nothing has been done."

About that time, a woman in a white uniform came in and hung up a new IV bag. She glanced at the monitoring equipment and seeing it not being used, took it with her. Mark's AtCon was vibrating so fast and so green that I could sense heat from it. "Mark, we can't help Bennet if we lose our composure."

"Fiona, can our AtCons tell us how hot something is?"

"Yes, at least I can tell what the ambient temperature is."

"See if you can tell what Dad's temperature is inside his ear."

"How far inside?"

"As far as you can get."

I went pea-size again and moved into Bennet's ear—also hairy and dry. Once I got past the hair, the channel got much smaller, so I got a little smaller. Finally figured I was as close to his eardrum as I could safely be and took a reading. "38.5 degrees Celsius. He feels warm to me." Being in a man's ear seemed weirdly intimate and I could not wait to get out.

"You're right. He's running a temperature. Something the monitors were supposed to check."

Bennet's eyes fluttered open. His head rolled slightly from side to side. His breathing was shallow. A container of water was sitting on his nightstand. He saw it. He struggled to raise himself and then pushed the button to raise the head of his bed. He reached one arm out for the water, but knocked it over. An orderly was walking past and heard the noise. "Mr. Soren, let me get you some more water."

A few minutes passed when he returned and held a glass of water with a straw to Bennet's mouth. He drank it all and asked for more. The orderly felt his forehead and left quickly.

He returned trailed by Ginger, my favorite nurse. "What's going on here, Mr. Soren?" She looked at the chart, looked again at the IV bag, and took his temperature. It pleased me that she wrote down 104.5 degrees Fahrenheit, which is 38.5 degrees Celsius. "Stan, get the monitors in here and hook him up for vital signs, EKG, and oxygen saturation. Right away!" "Mr. Soren, how do you feel right now?"

"Dizzy, tired, thirsty," he spoke in a whisper.

"Well, that all goes together. You are dehydrated. Up for one of my special cocktails? What flavor this time? I remember you go for the citrus. I'll get you one of those little umbrellas to put in your glass. I'm going to put your bed up a little more. There. Stan is going to hook you up to some monitors so you can't get away with anything. And I'll be right back."

Mark followed the nurse out the door. "Stay here with Dad."

While I waited, Stan returned and attached patches with wires to various parts of Bennet's body. He left and returned with the monitoring equipment that he stationed to one side. Soon, the telltale bleep-bleep signaled everything was working. I thought of Jennifer and wondered where she was now. She would be pretty old but maybe alive. How would I feel if it was her life in danger? I felt guilty that I had looked forward to Bennet joining the dead selves.

When Mark returned, he was calmer. "Thank God for nurses. I read over her shoulder. She went right to the medical records and even called up some references on her computer to check Woodson's recommendations and caught everything that I had worried about. She is talking to Woodson now."

Soon Ginger returned, flushed and angry. She had a colored beverage that she held for Bennet while he sucked it down with a straw. Stan came in with a tray of food—kidney bean salad, roll, chicken fried steak, mashed potatoes and gravy. On the tray was a paper cup with a white pill. Mark took a closer look at the pill. He was quickly mastering his sensors. He didn't like what he saw.

"That idiot doctor has ordered her to follow his recommendations. I bet that's Adderall—a stimulant." Mark was once again moving restlessly around the room, vibrating so fast that he hummed.

"Mr. Soren, could you eat some dinner if I helped you?" Ginger was spreading a napkin over his lap and took a seat on the edge of his bed. Bennet opened his eyes and coughed.

"I'll try." His head rolled slightly.

"Let's start with the mashed potatoes and gravy."

Ginger held a small bite of the mixture on a spoon to his mouth. Bennet did not respond. She pushed it gently across his lips. He parted his lips and let her slide the spoon inside and scrape off the food. About that time, the orderly returned.

"Gina wants you in Room 209—Mrs. Livingston is delusional again and thinks there are snakes in her room. She has the whole floor upset. Since you're the only one who can calm her, I'll feed Mr. Soren."

"Be careful that he doesn't choke on anything. His oxygen saturation is borderline and he is coughing some. Go slow." She put the plate down and rushed from the room.

We watched as Stan fed bites of meatloaf and kidney bean salad into Bennet's mouth. We saw no evidence that Bennet was chewing anything. After a few minutes, he started coughing and food flew out his mouth. Stan cleaned up the mess and noticed the pill on the tray. "Adderall. How stupid to not give him this first."

"Mr. Soren. Stick out your tongue for me."

Bennet made an effort to stick out his tongue. Stan tipped the paper cup so that the pill dropped on Bennet's tongue. Mark was hovering over Bennet as Stan encouraged Bennet to drink some more of the citrus concoction. All AtCon visual sensors were poised to see if Bennet swallowed the pill with the drink.

"Let's give that a little time to work and I'll be back to finish feeding you," Stan said over this shoulder as he left the room.

About that time, Jonas appeared. "What's going on? You called me?"

"Bennet's doctor here gave him Adderall to counter the effects of his antidepressant. And is insisting that they feed him a heavy meal while he is partially sedated and has a lot of congestion in his lungs. Mark is very upset, made worse because he can't figure out how to do anything to help his father. Can you think of anything?"

"For whatever it is worth, I understand your frustration, Mark. What specifically would you most want to affect?"

Mark was quick to answer, "Get that pill out of his digestive system, the one that's either in his mouth or working its way down his esophagus."

"Maybe we can make him cough it up. Like when you went down in his lungs," I said.

"You went down in his lungs?" Jonas could not conceal his amazement.

"Fiona, you are a sweetheart and brilliant to boot. It's worth a shot." Mark reduced the size of his AtCon and moved up into Bennet's right nostril.

"I don't believe that I'm seeing this," Jonas moved closer to Bennet's head. "Where are you now Mark?" he telepathed at twice the normal intensity.

"I'm in his throat, trying to irritate it. If I just had more mass or weight."

"Jonas' AtCon disappeared into Bennet's left nostril. His telepath was clear. "Let's both vibrate against each other, Mark. On three: one, two, three."

I hovered on Bennet's chest watching his throat. His eyes fluttered open; he took a deep breath and coughed. And coughed again. I heard Jonas message Mark, "I'm in his mouth."

"Get to the back of the roof of his mouth and see if you can get up into his sinus cavity," Mark sent the telepath with urgent intensity.

"Better yet, I'm going to teleport to the room. That worked. I'm out." Jonas was hovering near me.

"Mark, nothing came out of Bennet's mouth. He is trying to drink some water. Don't let him wash you into his stomach. Teleport to the room. Teleport now!" I watched as Bennet sucked deeply on the straw and swallowed.

There was no sign of Mark's AtCon. Bennet coughed again, loudly this time. He was struggling to breathe. Stan came into the room and placed a breathing tube in both nostrils and adjusted the oxygen. Bennet stopped coughing and lay back on the raised bed. The color in his face went from ashen gray to something more normal. His chest moved up and down more slowly. He closed his eyes and seemed to be resting. The monitor stopped bleeping so loudly.

"Well, we did our best. Now we just have to wait and see. The pill should be assimilated in about thirty minutes." Mark's AtCon appeared near the monitors. "Sorry if I scared you, I panicked and teleported to my home in Denver. Let Amelia know what was going on and got back as fast as I could."

"Jesus, I thought you were swimming in an acid bath of digestive juices. So what now?" I moved closer and enlarged my AtCon.

"Although I had to try, I am resigned to there being nothing I can do to help Dad. He is seventy-nine and has been complaining a lot about his life recently. I wish I knew what he wanted other than to not be resuscitated."

"There is possibly a way to find that out. Our pod mate, Valerie, could read live selves thoughts when she was alive. I'm not promising anything, but, like you said as you disappeared down his nose, it's worth a shot. Jonas and I will see if we can find her. Jonas, meet me back at the library."

And thus I decided how to resolve my lie of omission. Jonas now knows Valerie can read minds without the benefit of telepathy or consent. He and I are now on a level playing field with Valerie able to read both our minds. Ethically, I cannot ask her to keep my thoughts confidential, but not his. Shit. I never intended to be this honest. I lost my trump card with this move. Well, I still have my instincts and they are telling me that Jonas' obvious deflections mean he is hiding something.

CHAPTER 7

I suspected that Jonas would be curious enough to wait to talk to me about Valerie, but he was nowhere around the library. Nor could I find Valerie to give her a heads-up. So where is she? The microfiche archives were deserted.

I teleported to the magnolia tree where I saw Jonas' AtCon up the rise near the old barn. "Jonas, can we talk?" He was instantly at my side.

"Are you upset that I held back telling you that Valerie could read minds? My reason was to confirm that I could trust you, but then you made a pledge to us that I could not honor if I withheld what I knew about her mind reading." My recitation was well rehearsed and quickly delivered before he could interrupt me.

"It's a moot point, Fiona. Valerie is gone." Jonas' AtCon's glow went from blue to gray.

"How do you know she is gone?"

"I looked everywhere for her at Camden Yards. One minute she was right beside me and the next, she was just gone."

"Wait a minute. Camden Yards? How did you two get to Camden Yards?"

"Last night, just when you took off to check on Bennet, I was about to suggest that we all go enjoy the electric lights. Rather than let you spoil my celebration of our pod, I invited Valerie."

"Jonas, this is important. Play the entire conversation for me."

Jonas: Valerie, let's do something to celebrate. Let's go catch the baseball game between the Orioles and the Yankees. Blow off some steam and have some fun.

Valerie: Is that like cricket? And can you show me how to blow off steam?

Jonas: You bet I can. I am the best steam-blowing guy you will ever know. Here are the coordinates.

Jonas: Say, you are getting good at this, almost as fast as I am. Faster than Fiona. Follow me up to the very top section of seats where the lights are the brightest.

"That's it. I moved ahead of her AtCon and when I looked back, I saw that she had not moved and looked confused. I telepathed as forcefully as I could for her to come on. But she started moving away from me. I followed after her but she went faster and faster. And then she disappeared in the trees. I telepathed all around the area where I last saw her, looked through the trees, and came back today and looked. She hasn't been at the library either. I checked in with Victor to see if he or the other geeks had seen her."

"What are you doing here, Jonas? More specifically, what is the attraction up near the old barn?"

"It's really none of your business, Fiona. Better we try to find Valerie. Meet me at the library."

Back at the library, he assumed his hologram and sat at one of the large oak tables with his red-booted feet on display.

"Let's start off with a full disclosure—pod mate to pod mate," he telepathed. "I filled you in on all I know about her disappearance, now you tell me what you know about her mind-reading abilities, and any other special powers either of you has. You can skip any description of your power for deception; I think I'm well-schooled on that one."

I played back for Jonas the telepathed conversation that I had with Valiant/Valerie when she spoke about her ability to read minds and how difficult it was to be around live selves. I shared my brief telepath the previous day when I asked Valerie if Jonas was telling the truth when he made his promise.

"That's it. All I know and all that, to my knowledge, Valerie read from your mind. No harm, no foul. You may have a complaint that I did not tell you the moment we pledged to the pod. I apologize for that."

"I'm sure there is some complaint of greater substance buried in the amazing set of circumstances that you laid out, but it can wait. What do we do to find Valerie?"

"Let's start by looking around here, which would be the logical place to come if she was feeling scared and confused. One of the things I miss that surprises the hell out of me is the ability to leave a simple note."

We both toured the archives room recording all sensory input. I particularly checked the PCs and microfiche viewers to see if she was hiding in one of their holders—small places where film on spools rest. Nothing.

"Did you talk to all three of the Geeks Anonymous?" I asked.

"Vince Senior wasn't in the room when I was there. But she didn't like him and wouldn't have gone to him for help."

"Occam's razor. The simplest answer is most likely the correct one. She is still there. Let's look at your memory store for all visuals from the time you arrived at the stadium to the time that you left. When she arrived at your coordinates, she was about fifteen meters off the ground. That means she teleported into a wave of thoughts from the crowd below her."

"That would have been a bunch of Yankee and Oriole fans—as vehement and angry as any in baseball," Jonas replied. "How was I to know she could hear their thoughts?"

"OK, I'm getting your projection of what you saw. You appear to be moving across the crowd still at about fifteen or twenty meters when she draws back and up. She is trying to get away from the painful reads from fans. You would choose a Yankees game. Now you are coming toward her and she continues moving both away from the gate and higher. Freeze frame! Look closely. Do you see anything unusual? See there. Get a close-up on her AtCon. She has turned thirty degrees to the left and then paused. Slow speed now. She is rising straight up by the tree, but not in the tree. Freeze frame. See? She is fully visible with the tree in the background. She is not seeking shelter. Slow speed again. She is going straight up and out of your vision. You were searching the tree. What would be above the tree? Where was she headed?"

"Let's go find out." Jonas and I arrived at Camden Yards' main gate at the same time. We found the tree and her last position and looked to the left and straight up. We were staring at the lights over the scoreboard. We were over the bleachers. I telepathed, "Valerie. Valiant. Fiona wants you." Jonas had the sharper visual sensor and caught the movement of an AtCon. No larger than a golf ball, Valerie was lying in a pile of food wrappers under the bleachers just inside the main gate, directly below the scoreboard.

"Valerie. Are you all right? Can you move? Think something."

"Fiona. I may have let off too much of my steam last night. My AtCon's gyroscope is off-center. All my images in my memory store are blurred. I was afraid to teleport to a blurred image. My clock is set for a Peruvian time zone. I was so knackered, I decided to just hide here among the trash until I got better."

"And how did you know that you would get better?" Jonas asked.

"Well, I am already dead, so what else is there?"

Jonas' AtCon was vibrating and bobbing up and down in laughter—a badly needed break in tension.

"I'm going to telepath the image of the library right now. See it? Now go there!" Jonas went ahead and I followed when I saw her AtCon disappear.

She made it to the library outside and then hovered erratically on to the microfiche archives. I stopped Jonas so we could huddle. "Is she drunk from too much electricity?" I asked him.

"Most definitely. If she were not so distracted by the thoughts from live selves, I would have introduced her to the experience in modest increments. But don't worry. She just has a molecular hangover. I have weathered worse with no long-term effects."

"I wouldn't be so sure of that. It would explain a lot. She is in no shape to communicate with a dying man and his distraught son. Stay with her tonight and remember that she can pick up your thoughts even when you are not in telepath mode. Don't think anything that would upset her and don't leave her alone."

"I take it you are going back to stand vigil with Mark."

"Promised Mark that I would help out and he doesn't need to be alone either. If I am not back here in the morning, it will be because Bennet is not doing well."

"Don't forget that Mark is a married man." Jonas quipped.

"So are you."

NOW THAT I'M DEAD

CHAPTER 8

Back in Bennet's room, things were much as I had left them. Mark's AtCon was moving restlessly around the ceiling, since it is less an obstacle course than the floor. "Sorry, Mark. Valerie is still recovering from accidentally encountering a crowd of Orioles/Yankees fans at Camden Yards last night. Their thoughts were so hateful that she went into hiding. I don't think she is up to reading Bennet right now, but we can try later.

"Don't share that information with anyone, including your wife. Communications between dead and live selves is strictly forbidden and we put Valerie at risk if people learn of her gift."

Mark's telepath was more modulated and steady than it had been. "Of course. I understand.

"If Dad does not join us now, it is inevitable that he will. As long as he doesn't suffer, I'm not going to worry about him. I still have to plan for Amelia and me. We are now 'dead selves.' I'm still learning, but this is a kind of life. I still exist but in a much different form."

"How does this version of an afterlife compare with what you expected?" I asked.

"Jews don't believe in an afterlife, so I just assumed death was nothingness."

"Me too. I'm an atheist. So, what does your planning look like at this point? If I'm not being too nosy."

"Actually, I was hoping you would help me process my options since you know more than I do about my new state of being."

"I'm just one chapter ahead of you, but I'll do what I can."

We spent the next hour, thirty-three minutes and fifteen seconds reviewing the lifestyles of dead selves I had met, how to teleport and telepath, and what role physics played in our AtCon powers. Mark then asked about Jonas.

"How do you know who you can trust here? Specifically, why do you trust Jonas?" Mark asked.

"I don't have any reason to trust or not trust him. We met by accident in my old backyard, which turns out to be near where he once lived as a slave. Since that time, he was kind enough to show me the ropes. We both took on raising Valerie together when we realized her gifts were extraordinary enough to put the kid at risk. That led to forming a pod. One thing just led to another. Just as they did when we were alive."

"Except when we were alive we could see and read people's body language," Mark said.

"True, and how many people were shot by cops because they were black and didn't make eye contact? Fess up. Even most live selves don't read body language all that well.

"In our case, we trust each other because we both know and trust your father. But trust may not be as great an issue when you are dead. There is no property or wealth to protect. No one AtCon is more powerful than another. There is less to gain by deception when you are dead, but people lie for all kinds of reasons. I don't have a good answer for who to trust. But that was true when I was alive as well."

"And what is our relationship with the living?" Mark asked.

"Pretty much unchanged other than the inability to interact with them. We can go see them, hang around them, watch them go through their lives, but they cannot do the same. We don't lose them. They lose us. Are you feeling okay about Samantha's prospects?"

"She is in good hands with Kate and there is plenty of money to go around. Amelia tells me that she overheard Samantha talking about coming back to D.C. and what area she would want to live in. Sam is still close with our old neighbors and their kids in D.C. and Kate is well established in her career. Time will heal their wounds. Does time work the same for dead selves?"

"I suspect not. Here time has no real meaning because there is no ending that we know of. Jonas died in his prime but that was 149 years, six months, nineteen days, six hours, and thirty-eight minutes ago. I died at age seventy-six, three months, sixteen days, four hours, and twenty-two minutes ago. I am a neophyte dead self and an old woman. He is a man in his prime whose dead self has been around three times longer than your live one has."

"Most things that I would do in retirement—attend theater, concerts, sporting events, travel, and have conversations with like-minded others—I can do as a dead self. And teleporting beats the dickens out of cars, planes, and trains. And not knowing the language is not a hitch. Telepathy is not about language, just thoughts. Letting another dead self know where to find the pyramids works the same in every language. As soon as I learn more and find a good travel companion, I'm making a list of places I want to see—like the top of Mount Kilimanjaro, Morocco, and, most of all, Tahiti. For me, the afterlife is like a Garden of Eden—everything I need and a lot of what I want."

"No offense, but I'm not old and debilitated. I'm in my prime with a fascinating career where I excelled. I had the world at my feet. What do I do now? Am I supposed to replace my life as a famous neurosurgeon with a trip to Tahiti?" Mark's distress was palpable.

"I see your point. Death takes away more when you die young. I'm sure that Jonas and Valerie would welcome you and Amelia to join us, at least until you get something figured out. That way you have companions and resources until you get your bearings."

"Fiona, thanks. Until now, I felt, well, grim. Death is a tough sell, but with help, we might find a way to make something out of it. Could I ask a big favor? Would you stay with Dad so I can teleport to Denver and share this with Amelia? This would go a long way toward helping her acclimate. She isn't as strong as I am."

"Sure, babe. Take off. I told my pod I would stay here as long as Bennet was at risk. Anything I should pay close attention to?"

"It's all being monitored. If he experiences any distress, Ginger will know what to do."

"I'll be right here when you return."

With Mark gone and Bennet resting, I noticed the television on the wall was on with the sound turned down. I increased my sound sensitivity to watch the news. Dead selves without TV lose track of what is going on in the world. An hour later, I understood why we didn't watch. How could so many people get so much so wrong? Has the news always been this depressing?

Death has left me more aware and sensitive, more engaged with the world than I ever felt as a live self. Is this something peculiar to old people who die after living with diminished capacity for a time? Do we lose touch with life—its smells and sounds, the messiness of people in our lives—while we wait to die? Newborns need to be touched by humans to thrive. I wonder if that is also true for old people. Everyone loves a baby, but who wants to caress an old, liver-spotted hand? No one at Potomac Gardens at least. That's what latex gloves are for.

About that time, Bennet's monitors started bleeping. He was jerking a little and his eyes were open. An orderly I didn't recognize came in and left quickly. A few minutes later, Ginger was by his side.

"Mr. Soren, Bennet! Can you hear me? I'm going to raise your bed a little. There, can you tell me how you feel?" Ginger was shouting in his face. Then I realized I needed to readjust my sound sensors.

Bennet was making an effort, but was choking and coughing. Ginger raised his bed still higher. "Phillip," she called loudly. "Give me a hand."

When the orderly returned, Gina ordered him to stand beside Bennet's bed and make sure he didn't fall out.

She left for a minute and returned with an atomizer that she held up to Bennet's nose. "Take a deep breath, Mr. Soren. That's right. And another one. Good boy." By the time she had finished, Bennet's chest was moving and the monitors were making the rhythmic sounds that I now associated with an all-is-well state.

Ginger raised his bed a little, checked the monitors, and adjusted the oxygen. She listened to his lungs with a stethoscope. "I'm going to call his personal physician, Dr. Edison, and let him know what we have done. He may want to take him to a hospital and intubate him. Stay with him until I get back."

I retreated up to the ceiling and hovered just above the TV on the wall. When Ginger returned, she had a needle and syringe. She addressed the orderly again, "Dr. Edison wants him to have a different antibiotic and said that if we give him any antidepressants or stimulants, he would close the damn place. I will make that entry in Soren's records and I want you to write up what you witnessed and give that to me so we have everything documented. Dr. Edison is on his way."

Phillip asked, "Do you think he is dying? Should we call someone?"

"I will call his daughter. She is in Denver, but I have her cell. You write up your case notes and file them. Then keep a close eye on the monitors at your station and let me know if anything changes—for good or bad. I won't leave until he is stable."

How lucky I was to go so quickly. Poor Bennet. I wonder if it hurts. Ginger didn't exactly say whether he was dying or not.

I checked the time—11:30 p.m. (EST). Ginger's shift was probably over at 11:00. What if they take him to a hospital? Should I stay here so I can tell Mark where he is or go with Bennet? Damn. It would not do for Bennet to die and be alone, scared and discombobulated like I was. Would he come back here in response to the death threat? Or somewhere else? Hell, we could lose him somewhere in the vast reaches of metropolitan D.C. I have to stay with him, no matter where he goes. I wonder if I could telepath Valerie from here?

I gave it a try and waited three minutes. Tried again and waited three minutes. Just as I was going to try again, the monitors started up with the bleep sound that signals distress. Ginger came in with the second nurse right behind her.

"There is a DNR order, but let's make sure that his airways are clear." Ginger bent low over Bennet, blocking my view. When she straightened up, the monitors were silent, showing the dreaded flat line and buzzing the monotonous tone.

I shifted into my hologram projection and looked for Bennet's AtCon. I didn't see it. I was close to panic. To lose Bennet on my watch!! Then I heard him.

"Fiona, my dear. I thought you were dead."

The voice came from above my head to my left. There was a small AtCon hovering and giving off a pink glow. I turned my face toward him, "Bennet, old friend. We both are dead now. Please don't be scared. Mark will be here shortly. Just stay where you are until Potomac Gardens does its thing."

"Fiona! Where are you?" Jonas was telepathing from within the room.

"I'm here, Jonas. You are looking at me. Why are you here?"

"Valerie was sleeping it off when she suddenly expanded in size and telepathed "Fiona." I assumed that you had tried to reach her and was in trouble. And from the looks of you, something horrible happened. God, you are ugly."

"Well fuck you very much! This is my seventy-six-year-old image, the one that Bennet would recognize. Bennet just died. His AtCon is right behind you near the light fixture."

"Hello, Bennet. You can call me Jonas; I'm a friend of Fiona and Mark. Speaking of which, where is Mark?"

"He teleported to talk to Amelia."

"Mark is here too?" Bennet's telepath seemed strong.

"Bennet, most newly dead selves are very upset when they discover that they have died. We are here to reassure you that your experience is normal and everything is going to be all right. I'm going to get smaller and come up there to be closer to you. There, now. I'm right here." My hologram sat on the edge of the light fixture, with legs crossed and leaning back in an assumed pose of casual lounging.

"Cool. Nothing hurts. How do I make myself move around?" Bennet seemed in complete charge of the room.

"You just think in your mind where you want to be and presto there you are. Try moving around in the room until you get the hang of it."

Bennet's AtCon hopped from point to point and ended up in my hologram lap. "Fiona, I really missed you when you died. So this is where dead residents go—to haunt their rooms. A bit confining but, what the hell."

Jonas looked like he wished he were somewhere else. "Actually, Bennet, you can go anywhere that you can visualize or have latitude, longitude, and altitude coordinates for. Anywhere. But this room is where Mark will be meeting you, so best you stay here."

Bennet looked at me and asked, "Who is he?"

"I'm the man who took a dive into your nose to help Mark get you to cough up a dangerous medication. We both narrowly escaped getting swallowed and digested by you."

"Were you successful?" Bennet asked.

"Are you not dead?" replied Jonas

"Oh. Well, thanks for the try. I'm sure you meant well."

"Meant well? Are you saying that you preferred death?" Jonas' AtCon was taking that shade of blue reminiscent of a blue-gray rain cloud.

"When you are old, like Fiona and me, living is such a drudge. I ache when I totter in my slippers; I can't eat any of my favorite foods, smoke, drink, or get an erection. The kindest thing I can do for my loved ones and society in general is just get the heck out of the way before everyone's last memory of me is this mean-as-a-snake bastard who is paranoid and sullen, smelly, and disgusting. And consuming more than his share of the GDP in health care costs. I'm delighted to be dead even if this right now is as good as it gets. This is heaven! Nothing hurts and I can fly around the room!"

"Fiona, present your other hologram for Bennet. The one where you are riding a bike in Rock Creek Park." At that point, Jonas reveals his hologram and parades around the hospital room fairly strutting. The jerk is upset with my appearance.

"Another time, perhaps. I think I'm done here."

I teleported back to the library and checked on Valerie. Still sleeping. I thought about spending the night in the magnolia tree, but didn't want to leave her alone. I sighed and found a corner on a high shelf in the microfiche archives to hover over. I was so angry with Jonas and Bennet. How would these two ever work together?

And Mark. How long does it take him to explain AtCons to Amelia? I have spent days trying to help first one and then the other. I haven't had a decent night's sleep in three days at least. Let them work it out on their own.

I clicked through my memory store and replayed the day in Rock Creek Park again. It was a perfect day, a day when my daughters were teenagers, but were content to do something with me. And I rode the bike well instead of being a klutz and leaving my daughters rolling their eyes and laughing at me. The wind blew through my hair, the sun shone warm on us, and the emerald green leaves formed a cool canopy. It was like flying. My girls and I, flying three abreast and singing Linda Ronstadt's "It's So Easy." Too bad that they are such ungrateful brats and that I was never good enough for them. Maybe there would have been more good memories.

CHAPTER 9

"Fiona, wake up. You don't want to miss this." The telepath came from Valerie. There were no outside windows in the archives, so I asked for time and weather. It was 6:30 a.m. (EST) and 22 degrees Celsius with clear skies. A beautiful summer day. So what could I be missing at this ungodly hour of the morning?

"Look over by the study area."

There were three adult male holograms draped over various pieces of furniture. Jonas was the only one I recognized. He was stretched out on what everyone now viewed as his sofa, Stetson over his face and boots propped up on the sofa arm. The second man looked vaguely familiar—lean build, athletic, mid-forties and lying on a study table flat on his back with arms out flung. The third man was younger, in his thirties. He had a slight build, almost delicate hands, black curly hair, and that scruffy stubble that movie stars favor.

"Valerie, who are they?"

"You do not recognize Jonas?"

"Of course I do, I mean the others. Who are the others?"

"They said their names were Bennet and Mark Soren, but I am not sure which one is which. They woke me a few hours ago when they showed up in a state of electrical inebriation, meaning they let off way too much steam."

"Are you back to normal now? If so, meet our guests: Bennet Soren, a physicist, and Mark Soren, a medical doctor. They are father and son, although they could easily pass for brothers in their holograms. I have only seen them as AtCons, so can't help you out with which is which."

"Fiona, would you show me how to project a hologram?"

"Right now? Oh, okay. You have asked before and I've put you off.

"First, just project a picture. Imagine a memory of you and make a picture from that memory. Think about it like you're sending a telepathic message.

"Okay. There it is. I have it—you as a boy with shaggy hair, black jeans, and a tee shirt with food stains on the front. Now, show that boy moving around, doing something and send me that moving picture. There it is. You're juggling little bags of something in the air. You're pretty good.

"Now stop juggling but keep the boy and have him do something else, like walk over here and sit down next to me. This will not come from your memory but your imagination.

"You did it! And it is in your memory store, so you can go back and practice until at least the first steps are automatic. Applying your imagination to new movements for the hologram is the hard part for me. I still don't do that well. I wonder if it's just me. I was pretty uncoordinated and clumsy as a live self. My athletic and graceful daughters frequently made fun of me."

"But how do I change to a girl and make my clothes different if I have no memory to work with?" Valerie as a boy hologram evoked a motherly pang. She was so thin and shabby and, truth be told, a little dirty.

"Hmmm. That will take more time. I promise that I'll give you a makeover before day's end, but now I'm going to check something out before the guys wake up. Will you please stay here with them?"

I teleported to the old barn where I've frequently seen Jonas. It was once a tobacco barn where leaves of tobacco are hung across sticks that are laid across wooden beams. There are big cracks between the boarded walls so air can circulate to dry or cure the tobacco. The old wood has a silver sheen that gives the structure a ghostly ambience enhanced by missing boards and rusted metal roof. It must date way back.

I moved slowly through a hole in the side and toured the interior using my visual sensors. The sun shining through the openings between the boards cast bright stripes of light across the dark interior. It definitely is a long-term home for one or more large birds—the owl I hear from the magnolia tree? I adjusted my sensors to 4X magnification to find any markings or tracks. Vines had grown inside where they could get sun, obscuring a lot of the earthen floor. Barn debris littered much of the rest. Groundhogs had burrowed dens in places. Rusty nails protruded through rotten boards. But there was no sign of any human activity.

I toured again using my olfactory senses. The unmistakable smell of tobacco was dominant. It reminded me of my uncle's pipe tobacco. I also caught the stench of the owl's nest and its droppings, the earthiness of rotted wood and damp earth, and then something strange—a faint odor just along the outside edge of the barn where there was a round depression about four feet in diameter. I had read once about cadaver dogs and how they can pick up the scent of human remains fifteen feet underground long after decomposition had ended. The smell they track was from the ketones, sulfur, and calcium oxide. Almost any dog could detect the scent. I wasn't sure how my olfactory senses compared to a dog, but sulfur and calcium oxide were registering on my olfactory sensors. The abandoned   barn took on a sinister cast that contrasted sharply with the bright sunshine outside. It brought back memories of my recent meeting with my father in our ancient home. A breeze lowered the temperature around me. I steeled myself to take my time and be thorough

My vision sensor's X-ray setting that lets me see through book covers didn't work that well. I could see only down through about a foot of dirt to pick up shadows of rocks and bricks. Moving closer to the bricks, I noted that they were fit together in some places and scattered in others. Scattered bricks would come from a wall. The fitted bricks are still a wall. What has a curved brick wall that starts above ground and goes below ground? A well. This was the site of a well. Why would a tobacco barn have a well? It wouldn't. The well dates back longer than the barn. This was a well for a home. Not Jonas' home, which was farther down the slope, so it must have been the site of the old well for the main house. Huh. There is something strange in the old well of the plantation house.

"What are you doing, Fiona?" Jonas startled me.

"Looking at an old dilapidated tobacco barn. With an owl's nest in the rafters. And a body in the well."

"Ah, yes. The earthly remains of Master Demerson."

"And how did they come to be there? Seems like a strange burial plot for a man of his status."

"It was not his choice."

"Can you tell me more about Mr. Demerson's demise?" I projected my hologram wearing my jeans low on my hip, sandals, and a T-shirt.

"Why do you ask?" He projected his hologram dressed in jeans, tee shirt, and Docksiders boat shoes. The man has good taste in footwear.

"I want to know if you killed him; how did you do it? How did you interact with the natural world to kill Demerson?"

He laughed—deep baritone laugh. I heard the tone of his voice! Valerie had said something about teaching me to sing and I had paid no attention.

"My killing him holds no interest for you? Just the physics of it?"

"He needed killing and I hope you did it, but that's in the past and of no use in the future. But I could learn a lot by knowing how you did it." I said, trying to keep on-topic when what I really wanted to know is why I could hear his voice, not just the meaning of a telepathed message.

"I witnessed the murder, by a human, so sorry to disappoint. The old bastard had hidden gold and silver coins in the well during the war—the Civil one. He left it there rather than pay his creditors. Eventually, after losing the farm on a gambling debt, he came back to the old well to get his money and start a new life in St. Louis. I was shadowing him as I always did back then."

"It was a moonlit night. He used the well roof supports to rig a winch and a harness so he could lower himself fifteen feet into the well, but he wasn't strong enough to crank himself up with all the bags of coins. Easy to drop in, but strenuous to haul out. So he had to make several trips. He wasn't the stallion that he once was, so on what was probably his last trip, he was pretty exhausted. He threw the last bags over the well wall and then reached to pull himself over the wall when his hag of a wife brought down an ax on his hands. Blood started spurting and he just hung there, dangling in his harness. She then took a wide-arc swing with that ax and severed the rope of the winch; he vanished down the well where I could hear him screaming in pain, as could his better half. But she wasn't done with him. She poured kerosene on the wood roof of the well and the back porch to the house and set it all on fire. The house burned to the ground and rubble fell into the well hole. Last I saw of her, she was on horseback with the money tied to the pommel of that red-tooled fancy saddle of his.

"Folks just assumed that Demerson burned the house down and ruined the well out of spite. Someone saw his wife board a stagecoach going west and rumor had it that they had left town just ahead of the tar and feathers. No one looked for him after that.

"Now here comes my part in all of this. I knew that Demerson was probably dead and his AtCon was in the well. I also knew that no light could get in and chances were he would think that the dark and dank was normal for being dead. I telepathed to him that I was the devil and that he would now pay for his sins. Every night I would come here and talk to Demerson, mostly reciting in detail some act of meanness he had done to someone. On occasion, I recited scary passages from the Bible. If he tried to communicate, I threatened him with immediate dispatch to hellfire and brimstone."

"How long did this go on?"

"Fifteen years, six months, fourteen days, and seven hours. That's how long he owned me. And that's how long I owned him."

"Is his AtCon still down there?"

"Don't know. When they built the tobacco barn, they filled the well. Then when this area built up, the underground springs and streams dried up and I noticed the ground sinking some. Lately, I have telepathed him pretending to be God come to save him, but get no response."

"You pretended to be God?"

"Well, you gave me the idea."

"When you laugh now, I can hear your voice."

"Something I learned from Miss Valerie. Now walk with me to the walnut grove. I have something to show you."

I took his hologram arm as a way to gauge my speed and we made walking motions to the cluster of four old trees and six samplings. Near the edge of the grove, he motioned me to follow him to a tangle of vines and briars. "Look, see the stones? That was my fireplace. From that bush to that sapling and five meters from the fireplace mark the boundaries of my house, including a front porch with two steps. Israel was pretty proud that our house was up off the ground and had a plank floor. Come wintertime, I would stuff grass and straw up under the floor to keep the cold from coming through those walnut slabs. Using the wood from an old tree that I had to clear to get space for the cabin got me my first beating from Demerson. He was pissed because I got the benefit of his tree."

"Is it time to put Demerson behind you?" I asked.

"Almost. I still hate him for taking my family from me. "

"I've been thinking about what may have happened to them and why they never came back here. Slavery ended about the same time all over North and Central America. They could only have spent a few years in slavery before being freed. Israel would have tried to get word to you and, upon learning you were dead, she would not have any reason to come back here. Maybe it's a sign that they fared better where fate took them. The sonofabitch did them a favor in spite of himself."

"It's hard to think that they could be happy without me."

"Time heals the wounds of the living, but not so much the hurt of the dead, Jonas. You have reason to be happy for them. Find relief in that."

Jonas looked away toward the barn and then back to where his cabin once stood. "Let's see who can move their hologram up the hill the fastest." Jonas started jogging up the hill.

I gave up after falling in the grass and seeing my hologram arm spin off into the air. My AtCon got me the rest of the way to the magnolia tree where I had a ringside seat to an exhibition of superb hologram motion by Jonas. He really looked natural as he walked slowly up the hill, stopping to wave to me.

Up in the magnolia tree on our favorite branch, we changed the conversation to something more current. "Were the guys up and about when you left? " I hoped he would volunteer some summary of the night's events.

"Yeah. Mark had to run off to be with Amelia, but before he teleported, he and Bennet applied for membership in our pod. Valerie has lost all power of communication around Bennet, so we only need your okay. I'm for it."

"You want them in our pod? I thought you didn't like Bennet."

"I don't like Bennet around you. Otherwise he is first-rate. Funny as hell. I don't know who enjoyed last night the most— uptight Mark or Bennet. Once I showed them how to hologram, they almost forgot they were dead. Both of them tied one on."

"You need to join a 12-step program. Really. You can't be spending so many nights getting high on electrons."

"You were mad at me last night, weren't you? I can tell because when you are mad—rather than just being a thoughtless, bossy, shrew—your AtCon vibrates and rotates ten degrees to the left and then ten degrees to the right. Back and forth. The faster it rotates, the madder you are."

"It wasn't just you, Jonas. I was mad at Mark and Bennet as well. And don't ask me why. I was also tired.

"Wait a minute. I'm thoughtless? I will own that I'm bossy. And a shrew. But I didn't think that I was thoughtless."

"You are when you don't remember how much people care about you. Like when you just take off on mysterious errands with no explanation. Of course, that stuff doesn't bother me, but it upsets Valerie."

"I promise that I will never upset Valerie again. Are we good?"

Damn! He has teleported out of here without a by your leave! How rude!

NOW THAT I'M DEAD

CHAPTER 10

Back at the library, Valerie and Jonas were in hologram forms, sitting at opposite ends of the sofa, reading. Valerie had the appearance of an emaciated, vacuous model. She was wearing a dress with strategic cutouts and enough eye make-up to scare a raccoon. "Valerie, what?"

"Well I got tired of waiting! You never have time for me, so I have to do things on my own. Besides, Jonas said he likes it."

"Is that what he really thinks? If it is, he may be brain damaged by all the electrical binges."

"No, he thinks I am cool but he does not like skinny models. He thinks I need more breasts and a bigger booty because black men like nice booty and big legs. But he did SAY that he likes it." Valerie rose from a sitting position to stand briefly on 5-inch stiletto heels that laced up her skinny, incredibly long calves. She took one step and fell back into the chair, losing her hologram right leg.

"Valerie, let's start the makeover now. Do you have other pictures from the magazine that guided your current look?" Valerie nodded her hologram head and it also fell off. "Project some head shots so we can pick a hairstyle for you."

Jonas switched to his AtCon and teleported away while Valerie and I combed through ads until we found the perfect look. An hour later, thick glossy black bangs and a straight geometric cut--long in the front and short in the back--accentuated her long neck and delicate facial bones. With the addition of warm brown eye makeup from another ad, her naturally high cheekbones and long neck were now graceful things of beauty. With every flourish, her smile widened and my spirits lifted. How did I miss doing this with my own daughters?

She found a frilly, ruffled pinafore in summer colors and matching ballerina flats. I suggested that she also have in her memory a nice pair of jeans, sneakers, and tee shirt made for girls. Never know when one will be outdoors roughing it. We added some jewelry—earrings and bracelets. I dodged the breast issue for the moment, leaving her body as it was—a slightly built, flat-chested, and lean boyish form.

"Okay, let's go to the restroom where there are mirrors and see what you think."

Valerie assembled her hologram first in the girly outfit and then the jeans—taking long looks in the mirror. "I look like a girl in the ruffles—a skinny girl, but a pretty girl. In the jeans, I look like a boy."

"Add some pink lip gloss and a touch of rouge to your hologram. And get tighter jeans and one of those knit jersey things with wide horizontal stripes in pink."

"Wow, that makes a difference. My face is pretty!! I have a shape!"

"Yes, it is delicate, almost ethereal. You remind me of Audrey Hepburn, a popular movie star. As I recall she was pretty flat-chested as well."

"But men like her? Jonas does not like women without lots of breast meat."

"Well, that's just Jonas. Different men have different tastes in women. Besides, it's more important for a meaningful relationship that your man is more interested in what's inside your AtCon, not what you look like. Especially since we are talking about an imaginary hologram, not even a real flesh-and-blood body.

Actually, it is equally true for both. Ignore Jonas. Unless he's the one you want to be with when you feel sexy. Is he?"

"Oh no. Jonas is like my father. I like Bennet. Are you going to let Mark and Bennet join our pod?"

"Sure, it was always in my mind that they join us. I know we can trust them and they'll be invaluable assets to our research. Did Mark mention that he uses nanotechnology in his medical practice? And Bennet can take the lead on our research into particle physics. By the way, where is Bennet?"

"He is trying out his teleporting skills in his AtCon. He is supposed to come back here by nightfall. What kind of girl does Bennet like? Can I ask him?"

"Generally, a girl, or boy, shows interest not with words at first, but by little things they do. Like they find reasons to be near the other person and engage them in fun conversations. They'll try to learn more about each other to find the inside things that they like. Once they know they like the inside spirit of the person, then that kind of makes them feel sexy. Sometimes. Truth, you can read men's minds and that worries me. You will always know what they are thinking and what men think can be ugly. You should be prepared for disappointment, but your gift also assures that you will find true love. Or at least a connection with someone you can trust enough to explore a more intimate relationship. Better safe than sorry."

"Are you going to help me with that as well? What happens when a boy finds out that that I'm also a boy?"

"Short answer? Yes, I will help you. The long answer is to talk with Papa Jonas. For now, take it slow, just enjoy being a girl, and practice your hologram motion. No sexy feelings for a while. Promise?"

"Promise."

"Now do something for me. Explain how Jonas can project the sound of his voice now when he telepaths me."

"It is a lot like projecting a hologram. You have to remember the sound of your voice or a voice. That is hard for the AtCon because our voices when we were alive came out from under our ears, so we heard a voice different from what other people heard. It's easier to remember some singer's voice that you liked or can play from your memory store. If you concentrate, you can project that voice when you talk and you can sing with it. Which is why it is best to pick a singer's voice."

"Can you sing?"

"Sure. Who is this?"

"I am hearing Patsy Cline singing "Crazy". It's not exactly her timing, but your voice is so similar to hers. Now telepath a message in that voice."

"Dear Fiona. I am a big fan of yours and I hope you will have a happy life . . . er, death forever."

"I'm glad I can still tell it's you talking to me. Valerie, you are so special—incredible even. We are so lucky that the Geeks Anonymous wanted to be rid of you."

"Let's get back to the microfiche archives room and see if Bennet is back. I want him to see my new look. We are supposed to talk about my experiences when my AtCon was mapping mother board circuits." Valerie tried walking in her hologram outfit and got only around the corner before she lost the projection.

Later Bennet, Mark, and Jonas joined Valerie and me in the microfiche archives. By that time, I was able to "talk" using Linda Ronstadt's voice. We immediately set up a time for Valerie to teach Mark and Bennet. To my surprise, the young man was Bennet's hologram, and the fortyish man is Mark's actual appearance at time of his death. Valerie and Bennet's holograms make a cute couple.

With Jonas officiating, we took a formal pledge to protect each other and work toward mutual benefits and organized our work around two main tasks—how to expand the functionality of our AtCons and theories for puzzling questions about the afterlife. The latter was my suggestion. Bennet, Mark, and Valerie would work together on the first task. Jonas and I would work together on the second. Now he has to either lie or tell me more about what he knows.

In both cases, we would look for ways in which other dead selves, such as the Geeks Anonymous or dead physicists could be involved. No one would share pod information until the entire pod voted on disclosure. That included Valerie's ability to read minds.

I was the happiest I can remember being. I had friends who felt like family. I had my human voice back and could hear the sound of other voices. We were slowly recovering many of our lost abilities. If only we could learn how to manipulate tools, buttons, and switches!

The evening ended late. Mark teleported back to Denver, but Bennet took shelter at the library, reading long into the night with Valerie nearby. She was the only one of us who heard the faint echo within her AtCon.

"THEY ARE DOING IT AGAIN."

NOW THAT I'M DEAD

CHAPTER 11

"Valerie, are you sure that you did not inadvertently pick up thoughts from someone around you? You know, like on the other side of the library partition?" I asked while trying to clear my head of a dream that featured Jonas.

"No. This did not come from a human—dead or alive. There was no person attached to the telepath. It was like those recorded messages that come from computers—soulless and devoid of personality. No accent, no tone. But clear."

"Wait, let's get the guys in on this conversation so you won't have to repeat it."

"I do not want Bennet to think that I am odd." Her AtCon was vibrating nervously.

"Honey, you can't go into any relationship being ashamed about who you are."

"I thought the clothes and makeup were about making me into someone I am not."

"No. It's about making what you are prettier, not changing that. We brought out the girl in your personality so she can be seen.

Like me. I have boy in me. I wear boy clothes and do boy things that reveals the boy in me"

"Like saying 'Fuck' and taking down the Geeks." Jonas appeared wearing an Orioles baseball cap, a Nationals tee shirt, and a pair of Redskins sweatpants.

"Well, I like to think that saying 'Fuck' is more a diva thing than a boy thing. You been shopping on the Sports Fanatic website? Help me out here. I'm trying to make the point that a lot of what you see as boy and girl affectations are just social customs. There is nothing preordained about that stuff."

"But my penis is preordained, is it not?" Valerie was not letting up on her big concern but Jonas saved the day.

"Sort of, as an alive person, but not as a dead self. You have no body at all now—meaning that you have no penis. You can create a hologram with whatever body parts you want. But you can't change who you are as a person or your memories. What makes Fiona so attractive is not that she has such a great hologram body, although she does have a pretty great body, but she is such an interesting person. Interesting people are usually smart and curious. And pay attention to those around them. And have eccentricities and odd points of view. And talents."

"Like me! I am very interesting and talented and Bennet says that I am very smart not to have gone to school." As the idea attached, Valerie's mood brightened and her train of thought made another of its 90-degree digressions.

"Which reminds me, we need to have a pod meeting to discuss what I heard last night."

"We were coming to get you and Bennet in on this," I added. "Mark is in Denver, right?" I telepathed Bennet with a request to come to the study area. He appeared immediately.

"What's up?" Bennet was in his hologram form in a pair of black jeans and black T-shirt.

"He is gorgeous, is he not?" telepathed Valerie.

"Valerie heard a voice late last night that she doesn't recognize as human. Tell them, Valerie."

"I was hovering near the ceiling in my AtCon form. I was reading but getting sleepy. It was late—2:35 a.m. (EST). This faint voice reminded me of an echo or sound bouncing off another

86

sound wave. Like when landline phones would pick up a strong signal that distorted your voice and made it echo as you spoke into the phone."

"What did it say?" Bennet asked.

"'They are doing it again.' Just one time but it is in my memory store. Let me play it back."

I concentrated on opening my mind to receive as everyone else did. We all picked it up at the same time. "They are doing it again."

"Okay. Hmmm. Anything else going on around here? Maybe someone's dream or random thoughts?" Bennet asked.

"I can only pick up telepathed thoughts within a fifteen-meter radius. No one was that close to me. And this was definitely not a mind reading. That feels totally different."

"Could be something to do with the Geeks Anonymous' radio experiments—some wayward radio signal? Fiona and I will see what they are up to and if it is anything that could result in a radio signal bounced out here." Jonas stood up to signal the end of the meeting. "Bennet, let Mark know about this so he is kept in the loop. When do you expect to see him again?"

"The funeral services for Mark and Amelia are scheduled there this week. Then another week for Kate to put the house on the market. She is leaving all the furniture and personal effects in situ for now. They will all be back to D.C. at the end of July and Mark will be here during the day. I can't communicate with him unless he teleports back here, but I am keeping a detailed journal, so he will have all my thoughts and observations first hand. Meanwhile, Valerie will debrief me today on her experiences as a subatomic particle as our first step in looking at possible advantages or risks to downsizing our AtCons."

"Let's meet back here tomorrow morning at 9:00 a.m. (EST)." I closed out the session and Bennet went off with Valerie to the farthest reaches of the archives.

"Thanks for bailing me out back there with Valerie. How did I blow the obvious answer to Valerie's question about her penis? This must be what it's like to have a father in the parent picture."

Jonas adjusted his ball cap. "I never had any experience with teenagers. Valerie cries a lot. It is hard for me to think clearly when she cries."

"Well she is pretty immature for a nineteen-year-old girl and crying is pretty typical of adolescent girls."

"That's another thing. It is hard for me to keep her gender straight when she is not showing her hologram. I keep relating to her as a boy. That is how I first knew her and how I viewed her when I took her to visit the lights at Camden Yards—two guys hanging out."

"So now she is a guy with a feminine side. Big deal."

"But crying goes with that side. Why does she cry so much?"

"Hormonal. Which also goes with 'feeling sexy' as she puts it. All of those emotions were caught up in her AtCon when she died and are still playing out. And she has a ginormous crush on Bennet. You may have to give him a heads-up. He is a good man and would never take advantage, but, well, Valerie is so innocent and takes things so literally. And can read his mind to boot.

"Now let me share with you a list of points that I think our research needs to cover."

"Do you think we can do this?" Jonas asked.

"Figure out what explains some odd observations? Maybe. Don't know until we try."

"No, I mean raise Valerie. It's a big responsibility."

"The biggest. I raised my daughters alone as a single mom. They turned out all right, but they don't seem to like me that much. I think I was just lucky with them. I did my job okay, but I seemed to have lost them along the way. We aren't close. When they came to me about moving to Potomac Gardens, I didn't protest but it hurt me that they didn't invite me to live with them. Now that I'm dead, I can review all my memories as a mother--housework, cooking, taking classes, getting them to school, and rushing to work. I achieved my goal of being someone, but not a someone that my kids want around. I don't want to do that again. Help me be more thoughtful and not be so up in the task that I lose sight of people I love."

Jonas leaned close to my AtCon. "You know, it would be easier to comfort you if you weren't in that AtCon rig."

I hologrammed into my jeans and tee shirt. He put his arms around me and I tried to remember what that felt like. The imagined pressure of his muscles and warm flesh pressed against me. Slowly, the sensations came to me. I could feel him. I laid my head against his chest; I reached my arms around his back. I remembered why he always covered his back—scars from the beatings. I touched them gently, imagining ridges of keloid tissue under sensitive fingertips. Did he feel my hands? I tipped my head back to look into his insanely blue eyes but they were closed. He bent his head down and I remembered/imagined his lips on mine. We held a long kiss. When we parted, he opened his eyes and looked into mine.

"Eye contact is a very intimate interaction, Fiona Campbell. I hope it is the first of many." And as his finger touched my lips, "Touch and be felt. Feel and be touched. I invite you to share my present state of mind."

"I'm not ready."

"I'll wait."

NOW THAT I'M DEAD

CHAPTER 12

The Geeks had located their pod at an abandoned radio tower on an old World War II military airfield off of Croom Station road, not far from where my house and Jonas' cabin were. We decided not to reveal either our ability to telepath voice messages or that Valerie could read minds. Nor would we mention the addition of Mark and Bennet to our pod. Jonas seemed more interested in what the Geeks knew than in sharing information with them. I didn't argue since the jury was still out as far as the Geeks were concerned. He telepathed our request to be heard as we approached the tower.

All three of the Geeks were there. What the tower lacked in aesthetics, it made up in security and solitude. The brick building enclosed a small room at ground level with a spiral metal stairway to a round room about seven meters in diameter and twenty meters high. Glass panes encircled the elevated work space and provided an unimpeded view across the Patuxent River and miles of flat farmland and marsh. The enclosure also held impressive-looking equipment and electricity. Given my earlier run-in with the Geeks, Jonas was taking the lead in the discussions.

"Good morning. Thanks for seeing us. We had a strange occurrence about 2:00 a.m. (EST). Valerie, or Valiant as you know her, picked up a message that was not telepathed by anyone there at the library. She said that it sounded like it had a slight echo such as happens when there are radio signals interfering with a landline telephone. Does that ring any bells for you guys?"

"Victor sending. Was the message 'They are doing it again?'"

"Yep!"

"Victor sending. I picked it up as well. It's not anything we were working on and we don't know where it came from."

"Vince Senior sending. It could have had some connection to that big high-frequency radio wave last night."

"Jonas here. What radio wave?"

"Our sensors registered a giant, high-frequency radio wave about the time Victor heard the message. Can't say that there is any connection because we don't know what it is. We can say that it is not a radio, radar, television, telephone, or satellite-generated phenomenon that we recognize and we have been playing with most of them. It's way too powerful for that. We do know something about the phenomenon. In the past seven years, the Parkes Telescope in New South Wales has picked up eleven bursts with the same mathematical dispersion pattern as last night's wave. No one has figured out what they are, but they are powerful high-frequency waves coming a long way through space and packing a lot of energy."

"Fiona sending. If these super waves have been picked up for seven years, why don't we know what they are by now?"

"Vince Senior sending. These events are infrequent. The scientific community needs a certain sample size before they can postulate what something is with any acceptable degree of confidence. Eventually they will hit that magic number and tell us what they think, complete with all the folderol math that goes with that. It could be another seven years or longer. They see no need to rush to judgment. Toots, you would be amazed to know how many unexplained phenomena we have on record."

"How are you doing with your new communication system?" Jonas was trying to deflect Vince's "toots" reference before I went ballistic.

"Vince Junior here. We are working on two AtCon enhancements. The first is an e-mail system that would allow AtCons to access the Internet and send e-mails. We are using higher frequency radio waves at the molecular level where we can harness the energy from a chemical liquid or air diffusion. It is just a matter of time when we find the perfect medium to carry binary code between AtCons and local e-mail servers. That would let us send written messages to each other on local e-mail servers and, of course, search the Web. Once we accomplish that, we can have our own e-mail server that can interface with all other e-mail servers. We are making headway, but still have a few hurdles."

"However, we are close to having our own radio transmission system for a kind of telephone that uses Morse code. Right now, telephones are useless since we cannot project any sound. However, if we install Morse code in each AtCon's memory store, we could transmit telegraphed messages to that setting for converting telepaths to or from Morse code. This is pretty simple stuff and we are close to having it worked out. It would let us communicate across long distances and among multiple users simultaneously."

"Fiona sending. If you guys are right about your approaches to creating an alternative Internet and telephone system and AtCons have been around for ages, then why hasn't someone already done this?"

"Because we haven't had the science to do this until the last fifty years. This is Vince Junior."

"Fiona here. You are speaking of live selves, not dead selves. Of all the genius physicists, mathematicians, and scientists who have ever lived, how many are now dead? Galileo, Newton, Einstein, Dirac, Oppenheimer, and all the guys they debated with back in the early 1900s. They've been thinking about this stuff longer than you have and, although you do bring the benefits of the state of the art in computer science, I can't see Albert Einstein twiddling his thumbs for the last fifty-nine years, two months, six days, and twelve hours since his death."

"Vince Senior here. What's your point, Fiona?"

"My point is that we may not be on our own here. Think about it. There are a lot of things in place that we don't control but communications are a major deterrent to our ability to work together. What if the 'they' in the message is us? And what if the thing we are doing is organizing to better manipulate our environment and consequently, the dead world order?"

"Victor here. That's pretty paranoid. Why did only two of us rather than all of us get the message?"

"Fiona here. If an Internet already exists and all AtCons are connected to it, then the AtCons getting the message may have had their routers turned on and the others didn't. Then the super radio wave caused the message to jump to all open routers."

"Okay, then what would determine whose router is on or off?"

"Vince Junior here. A router would be like a tether to the main network of servers. Individual routers would be on to accommodate the network administrator who may want to update software, clear out viruses, or in our case read our memory store where everything we've done is recorded in great detail. I used to make sure that my employees were not violating security protocols by reviewing their computer memories at night when they weren't around and we did it monthly based on when they were hired. Valerie got the message as did Victor, who coincidentally died about the same time. Just saying."

"Vince Senior speaking. Jonas, what do you think about this?"

"Who knows? This is all speculation. And even if it were true, what could be done about it?"

"Fiona sending. For a starter, we can pay more attention to counterintuitive observations. Why are there not more dead selves around, especially Native Americans who were living here far longer than white folks? And the missing juveniles? And the scarcity of women in the dead self population. What's with that?"

"Jonas sending. You are forgetting that AtCons can be reduced in size so that they are very hard to detect. I'm not predisposed toward conspiracy theories when there could be a simple explanation of what Fiona calls anomalies."

"Fiona here. Give me a list of oddities that you have noticed and let me do some research on them, just to see if our perceptions have any basis in fact."

The Geeks Anonymous pod gave us a pretty comprehensive list of questions to guide our research and volunteered to search for the "router" that connected their AtCons to what Victor calls the Dead Web. I was determined not to lose the momentum that I had finagled during our discussion with the Geeks, so upon returning to the library, I proposed a plan. "It seems like our next step is to go through what we have as unexplained events, organize them by areas of knowledge/expertise, and see if anything falls out with Mark, Bennet, or Valerie's name on it. Then you and I will do the rest." But Jonas had something different in mind.

"Frankly, I want to mull this over and see if I can find flaws in our approach. I do better after I sleep on it. And I sleep better if I have blown off some steam."

"The last time you suggested blowing off some steam, we lost Valerie and I had a panic attack. Besides, if I went with you to a baseball game, I would feel like an enabler."

"Vince Senior was right about you. You are a drag. Tell me. When was the last time that you were high or had a buzz on?"

"My last night in my house. I drank as many martinis as I could and fell asleep in a patio chair."

Minutes passed and I thought what a fuck-up I was. This man is trying to flirt and have fun with me and I'm just a big, wet blanket of a dead woman. No wonder there were never many men in my life.

"I have an idea," Jonas said. "How about I take you out to a nightclub tonight? We will listen to some rocking good soul music in our comfy AtCon rigs and see how the other half lives."

"You're kidding."

"Hell no! I like a club in Silver Spring that is set up like an old-fashioned supper club. They serve really bad food and watered-down drinks but their bands are great. We can leave whenever you want if you don't like it."

I thought what a fool I would be if I passed this up. "Yes. Music would be the perfect way to let off some steam. Do you want to invite Bennet and Valerie?"

"Not this time. Just because I don't want to answer questions about our meeting. I will see you at these coordinates at 8:30 p.m. (EST). It's an address in Hyattsville." Then he was gone.

Unlike Jonas, I could not dismiss all that we learned just now. I was anxious to talk to someone about it. I hovered around the microfiche archives looking for an AtCon and spotted Bennet walking around in his hologram form all by himself.

"Getting some practice in?" I asked as I joined him in my hologram. "Mind if I join you? I need it as well."

"Fiona, my dear friend. You are so welcome. You and I have spent less time together dead than we did alive. Must find a way to play Scrabble without hands and get it on like in the old days."

"You do realize that the old days were just a few months ago, right? Time moves differently now, or is that my imagination? My existence as a dead self moves so rapidly from event to event. Is it the rapid change of scene when we teleport?"

"Could be. Without regard to Einstein's theory about relativity and time, humans measure time psychologically. When we are stimulated, time seems to pass quickly. And just the opposite when we are not. Our degree of mental stimulation probably accounts for the sense of time moving quickly in the afterlife. Which is why we need to have reliable internal clocks synchronized with absolute time that keeps us oriented."

"Wow! Something just came to me. A few hours ago during a meeting with the Geeks, I made reference to how long Einstein has been dead to the minute. How did I know that? Earlier when I called up information on him in my memory store, I could find nothing about Einstein that mentions his birth or death."

"Was time the context for today's recall?" Bennet asked. "It could be that our AtCons have different organizational schemes for storing and retrieving information. Humans typically organize information by subject—Einstein—or by time—when something happened. It is possible that given AtCons' concern about accuracy with reference to absolute time, we can look at any time interval and pull up everything that dead people did during that interval. As incredible as that seems, my research on the data-analysis capabilities of our AtCons indicates that it is possible."

"Fiona, I bet the time database is the originator's and must be one of the largest collections of data anywhere—all the personal data of every dead self. It would not be a difficult database set up. The Geeks could probably tell us how it could be done."

"Bennet, promise me that you won't say anything about this to anyone. You are the only person here that I KNOW that I can trust to be who I think you are. I especially don't trust the Geeks."

"As you wish, Fiona. You are probably right, but I can still think about it. Why would the originators want to keep those records? How do they use human activity organized by time interval?"

"If you figure that out, let me know. Meanwhile, let's see if we can slow dance in our hologram forms."

NOW THAT I'M DEAD

CHAPTER 13

The address Jonas gave me was one of the new upscale, artsy condominiums that featured retail shops or artists' studios on the ground floor and apartments above. I had read about it but never had any reason to come to this area. I was delighted by what I saw on this soft summer Saturday night. Jonas appeared right on time and joined me as I floated above the old-fashioned streetlight.

"Why are we here?" I asked.

"Do you like it?"

"Yes, I do. It's charming. Who lives here?"

"A couple by the name of Veronica and Louis Hedrick. They are regulars at this club and usually rent a limousine to ferry them there and back. Thought you might enjoy a drive through the 'hood and some intelligent conversation."

Soon a black limo pulled up and the driver made a call on his cell. The couple that came out was beautifully dressed. After they got into the backseat, another couple joined them from down the street. Jonas and I teleported into the car on his signal. We chatted via telepath from our positions on the backs of their headrests. I heard gossip about people I didn't know but learned that things had not changed much since I last had a social life. Wives still poked fun at their husbands and husbands still rolled their eyes at their wives. My attention was mostly focused on Jonas as he pointed out things along the way. The area was really building up and taking on a sheen of glamor and sophistication that did not exist when I moved to Prince George's County.

We hovered out of the limo at the club's entrance and went inside, trailing our adopted companions. "We can hang with them until they have had a few drinks then they'll start looking stupid because we are sober. Hopefully, the music will be playing by then."

Jonas led me to a banquet set up for six people and we positioned ourselves on its upper frame. I took in the soft lights, the colors of the women's dresses and the gilt-framed mirrors. A stage sat a half meter above a dance floor of polished wood. Soft music came from speakers surrounding the dining room. Plates of food floated past on huge trays expertly carried by servers dressed in black and white. I was glad that no one could see how astonished I was. As they ate things I recognized, I could recall the taste and touch of the food. "I can taste that steak that Louis is eating. You knew about this. That I could use my memory to enjoy physical pleasures of dining if I were stimulated to recall those memories."

"Well, of course I did. Actually, you are probably enjoying the steak by memory more than Louis is in reality. Pork ribs are probably better here and the fried chicken is the best. I'm sharing the guy's ribs over there and the lady's chicken right past him. Bon Appetit."

The roadies set up the stage and did a sound check. At 9:15 p.m. (EST), six musicians and three women singers mounted the stage and began their set with "When A Man Loves A Woman," Followed by "Dogging Around," "Tell It like It Is," "The Dark End Of the Street," and "Cry Baby"—all soul blues songs from the 50s and 60s. The place was jumping by 11:00 p.m. (EST) when Jonas telepathed, "Let's go where we can dance." Thinking that I was following him outside to a place where we could still hear the music, I was surprised when he said, "Meet me at Camden Yards, main gate."

Fans were crowding though the various exit points at the end of a double header. Jonas moved up to the lights, as I expected he would. Feeling a little manipulated, I nevertheless followed him. I could see numerous AtCons dive bombing the lights—seeing how close they could come and not hit one. "Isn't that dangerous?"

"A little. From the heat more than the unfettered electrons. They can't break anything and if they get too close, they will be repelled by the energy or they will go through it. That could reorganize their configuration."

I had more questions but he stopped where we were and said, "Now play "I Got A Woman" from your memory store. On the count of three: one, two, three." Jonas' AtCon literally rocked to the beat of the music. I mimicked him and it was just like dancing, but dancing in 3-D. We spun in place and then soared through the air, all in sync with the Ray Charles classic. He next cued up "Dogging Around," a slinky, four-beat tune where the fourth beat is extended for four beats. I followed his lead, moving when he did, pausing, and holding the beat when he did. We were dancing together—spinning in place and then spinning as we soared through the air. When the song ended, we were just centimeters apart and giving off a pink glow.

"I'm euphoric. It may be the lights or the music or just the freedom of movement, but I cannot recall a happier time."

But Jonas was gone. I am ready to follow him to the ends of the world, and he just disappears. That dude can really bust a mood.

I teleported back to the archives and fell into a deep sleep. I woke with a start at 4:43 a.m. (EST) with something my grandmother used to say resonating in my head. "A stitch in time saves nine." Its literal translation is that to mend an unraveling seam early on will save you from mending a much bigger tear. Or, early actions are efficient deterrents. What would that have to do with anything?

NOW THAT I'M DEAD

CHAPTER 14

I had not seen either Bennet or Valerie since the night before, which in Valerie-time is long enough for her to get into all sorts of trouble. Both were with Mark in the library study area. All three were projecting holograms. This time, Valerie was wearing a demure sweater and slacks outfit with flat sandals and just a touch of makeup. She looked so vulnerable and sweet. Is that anxiety I feel?

"Hi, where is Jonas?" I asked.

"He said to be here by noon for a meeting and then left. How did your research go yesterday?" Bennet was sending.

"Raised more questions than answers. But I'll wait until Jonas joins us to share my thoughts. Just so you know, we didn't let on to the Geeks that you and Mark are joining our pod or Valerie's mind reading capabilities. Nor did we mention our ability to telepath voice sounds, not just thoughts. Jonas can explain."

"Is Mark up to speed on everything?"

"Yeah, as soon as he can pick a voice for himself. I settled on Bruce Springsteen. Just need to memorize some lyrics and find us a karaoke bar now. At the moment, we are brainstorming Mark's problem. Kate and Samantha are scheduled to fly to D.C. Thursday, but Amelia is afraid to teleport outside the house. And she is claustrophobic so can't travel inside the luggage. Any ideas, Fiona?"

"Leave her there with the coordinates in her memory store. She will do it when she realizes she has to. We have more important matters to spend energy on."

Mark came to his feet, sending, "Wait a minute. Important problems like which famous singer's voice to appropriate? Are we in this together or not? How come my problem doesn't merit serious attention?"

"Because it's a non-problem. She will teleport herself to D.C. If she doesn't, she can easily be found in your old house; she sure as hell isn't going to teleport anywhere else. There isn't anything that can happen to her. She has to be able to communicate via telepath and teleport to function, unless she is just going to putter around the house like a lost soul for all eternity. You're not doing her any favors fostering any greater dependence on her part. No one helped you learn to teleport, right? We need you. And we may need Amelia."

"We will see what Jonas has to say about this." Mark was fairly hissing at this point.

"Here I am. I've been trying to get some information related to our visit with the Geeks Anonymous pod. Cool your jets, Mark. This meeting will be brief and more important than where your wife will spend the night."

Jonas summarized what we learned about radio waves and the mysterious message. "Then this morning I met with a group of Indians from the Powhatan, Piscataway, and Nanticoke tribes. They are the longest dead that we have here, but there aren't more than a few thousand active in the area as far as they know. They say that many Indians couldn't adapt to their AtCons and they were 'filled with despair and joined a spirit tide.' The spirit tide stems from their old legends about where the dead go."

I filled in with some of the other mysteries that bothered us, culminating with the one that I thought was the most threatening and obvious. "Right now, I am exhausted from trying to project to just four of you to share information. So, although we can teleport anywhere instantly, we cannot communicate to large numbers of people or over a distance of about twenty meters. Although we may number in the millions, this limitation puts our AtCons back to the day of the caveman where we can only act in small family groups."

"Geeks Anonymous are working on a communication system that sends Morse code across long distances and to multiple people simultaneously. They succeeded in creating a Morse code translation capability in an AtCon that translates the Morse-coded radio waves into telepathed messages and vice versa. They are also close to having a form of an Internet that would allow all AtCons access to the Internet. They have nearly worked out the science for this."

"Considering their progress in these areas of communication, I have to wonder what prevents others who have been dead longer to do it? What if each AtCon is already connected to a network that, like computers, can be accessed? This access would allow an intruder to read our memory store and delete or add memories. Whoever could do this is more advanced than our pods and thus has power over us. We don't know who that may be—dead physicists who got together and don't want any change in the power structure? Or some other dead self? A powerful corporation who is using dead selves for their own nefarious objectives?

"Whoever it is may be upset with us for 'doing it again'-- the 'it' being asking questions and looking for a way to be more powerful. That is what our research would accomplish— knowledge that would enable us to have more control over our AtCons. I believe that there is sufficient evidence of others out there who have found a way to control AtCons. There, I've said it."

There were several moments of silence before Bennet spoke. "If there is a visitation by a hacker into our AtCons that is done in cycles based on when death occurred, then the rest of us will be visited in turn, our memories reviewed and this conversation shared. If they are pissed about what we have done, they will go ballistic when they read this conversation where we are plotting against them."

Jonas spoke up, "Hold on. Vince Junior is here. He says that Victor's son is near death. Victor is with him and asks for help keeping watch."

"Mark, you're a doctor. You and Valerie have the most experience navigating at the particle level. Is there any possibility that you can help prevent Victor's son's death?" I was thinking as fast as I could about the ramifications of sending Valerie off to team with one of the Geeks.

"I can't say until I see what his condition is, but I could help Victor understand what is going on and Valerie's ability to read minds would be a great diagnostic tool that the live doctors don't have."

"I would like to help, either to keep him alive or protect him from anyone who would take him. I will go." Valerie stepped up, oblivious to Mark's revelation of her mind-reading abilities. I guess keeping that a secret was a lost cause anyway.

"Bennet Soren here. Tell Vince that I can join the Geeks Anonymous to work on their communications research. Perhaps a physicist would be useful."

"Jonas sending. Vince, let me introduce you to two new members of our pod. Dr. Mark Soren recently died and is a neurosurgeon well versed in nanotechnology. He and Valerie will be joining Victor to help out with his son. Dr. Bennet Soren, Mark's father and also recently dead, is a physicist and will return with you to the radio tower to help with your work on the Deadnet. Fiona and I are standing by if you have anything we can do."

"Vince Junior sending. Permission to speak and be heard, Mark and Bennet. Mark and Valerie, Michael Dubois is in room 918 at Children's Hospital, 4950 Sunset Boulevard, Los Angeles, California. I'm sending the coordinates. Victor will be there. Bennet, Jonas will give you directions for the radio tower. It's just forty-two kilometers from your location. I will meet you there and look forward to working with you.

"Jonas and Fiona, thank you for all your help."

Bennet and Valerie said their goodbye's before she joined Mark and teleported to Los Angeles. Shortly, thereafter, both Vince and Bennet disappeared. Jonas and I were alone.

"Looks like we have the right people in the right places and feeling the right amount of urgency. Speaking of urgency, what was so urgent last night that you had to abandon me in mid-sentence at the ballpark? You do that a lot." I could hear the annoyance in my tone and hoped that it communicated.

"I'm sorry if I was rude. I'll explain everything as soon as I figure it out for myself. Please be patient. I won't do it again."

"Okay. Take your time. I'm heading out to Los Angeles to get more detail on Michael's condition and to keep an eye on Valerie. Perhaps you should to the same at the radio tower. Make sure that Bennet settles in. We don't know much about his work style, but he seems like he has it together. I will circle back here in a few days. If you need me before then, you know where I will be. See ya, sport."

NOW THAT I'M DEAD

CHAPTER 15

Never having been to California, I was unprepared for the effects of palm trees, sunshine, dry air, and flowers everywhere. The hospital grounds seemed like an exotic tropical paradise. Even the highway median looked like a movie set. I let myself soak up the sunlight, sure that it would be better quality than what we had in Maryland. Despite the grim context, I felt light-hearted.

Room 918 was a private room. The one hospital bed held a pale thin boy with no hair. In a small daybed next to the window, a woman in her forties was lying on her side facing the wall. The back of her silk blouse and linen capris were slightly creased. A pair of Jimmy Choo pumps lay on the floor where she had slipped them off. Her two-toned blond hair fell stylishly across her face. The angular jawline and straight, delicate nose matched that of the boy's. This is a woman who commands attention on every stage. This is Michael's mother and Victor's lovely wife. No wonder he wants a way to communicate with the living.

I looked around the room and saw three AtCons. "Fiona sending. Mark? Victor? Valerie?"

"Valerie sending. We are all here, Fiona. Mark has not been able to see Michael's chart. All their records are electronic and we cannot log on. I am waiting for someone to come in whose mind I can read."

"Mark sending. Victor told me Michael was diagnosed with an inoperable tumor that has grown around his brain stem. They tried chemotherapy but that wasn't successful. They are considering thermal ablation using lasers, but that will be tricky as well. Imagine a tumor the size of a golf ball that has hundreds of blood vessels and nerves within it. These vessels are half the thickness of a human hair and the nerves are one-tenth the size of a vessel. Heat can kill cancer cells, but can also damage healthy tissue. If I can figure a way to get to the site, I can convert AtCon energy to heat that will kill cancer cells. I just don't know how long I can do that before I run out of energy."

"Mark, Fiona sending. Is it possible for you to use our AtCons as your thermal ablation device? Could we all go in with you and you put us in position, we generate the heat, then you reposition us until each one runs low on energy? Could four AtCons get the job done?"

"That's possible. I just don't know until I get down there. It would help to see the pictures, to know the exact location and size of the tumor. I can go in alone and do reconnaissance while he is out on the morphine. I want Victor's okay, though."

"Victor here. I hate to do anything without the medical history."

"Fiona sending. Mark, can you make the monitor register a problem so that his nurse comes in?"

"Victor here. I think I can. I can project electromagnetic waves that cause irregular EKG readings. Here goes."

"Mark here. Victor, it's working."

In less than a minute, a nurse came in and checked the patient and the monitors. As she made an entry in the patient records computer, Valerie read her thoughts and telepathed them to Mark. After she left, we got the bad news from Mark.

"Victor, it's not looking good. He is not scheduled for any treatment. They're just making him comfortable. He's a hospice patient. He's here to die."

"Victor sending. Do anything you can Mark. Anything."

"Mark sending. I'm going to enter one of the small veins draining blood from the eye and follow it down to the brain stem. I will take a look and project back to Fiona what I see and hear. Record that, Fiona. It'll be a makeshift MRI."

"Victor sending. Mark, let me go with you. I know exactly how that works using my X-ray visual sensors with my AtCon as the computer."

"OK, stay close behind me."

The two of them wiggled under Michael's eyelid and disappeared

"Valerie, can you tell if an AtCon came into the room? Can you sense it without your sensors picking up on it?"

"Yes. There is a vibration that I feel before I can pick up thoughts. No one can come into this room without me knowing."

"How's Michael's mother doing?"

"She is under a sedative and sleeping soundly. Not much going on there. The boy though is dreaming that he is flying with his father."

"How are things between you and Bennet?"

"He likes me. The inside me. He says that I am like a fresh breeze, pure and innocent. What do you think that means, Fiona?"

"That he appreciates your honesty and your decency. There is no evil in you. People can trust you. It's a good quality to have."

Soon, Mark and Victor were back.

"Victor, did you get everything? Can you project the pictures for me?" Mark was talking with great excitement.

"You bet. I'm going to increase its size and project on the white wall so I can enlarge it a lot. Here goes. This is the first shot from above. Now the second one at twelve o'clock, three o'clock, six o'clock, and nine o'clock. Now the last one looking up from the bottom. The tumor is irregular in size."

"Mark sending. Yes, we can easily access a large part of it and kill the cancer cells there quickly. That will reduce the pressure against the rest of the brain stem and give us more space to work in. If we can also kill the cells compressing this artery, the blood will flow better. And here is a section over here that we can take out easily. I think if we all go in we can kill half of all the cancer cells tonight. Then we give the cells time to die and go back in a few days to assault the rest. We will continue until we get as much as possible."

"Mark, are you saying we might save him?"

"Victor, no one has ever done this before. There are so many things that could go wrong—infection, his immune system attacking us, a blood clot or aneurysm that we set into motion. Don't get your hopes up, but I am one of the top surgeons in this field. If anyone can do it, I can."

"Fiona, Valerie, are you ready to go with us?"

"Fiona here. If we lose our patient, Victor has to teleport to the room instantly and project his hologram so Michael will recognize him and stay with him. Let's be prepared for all contingencies."

"Mark here. Follow my directions and refer to the pictures when we get to the site. You will have to adjust your visual sensors to make up for the loss of light. The vein we take from the eye is very small, and I will be using you like a tool so you must shrink your AtCon down to twenty micrometers going in. Then the vein we take to the tumor is larger, five millimeters. When I have you in position, I will say 'heat.' I will need temperatures of 60 degrees Celsius when we get to the site. Say 'ready' when you are at the right temperature. When you can't sustain the heat, say 'release' and move back and someone will replace you. Any questions? Then let's go!"

I followed Valerie and Victor brought up the rear in single file. I had never been this small before and had no idea what to expect. I could see globs of goo on Michael's eyelash follicles. Once under his eyelid, the light was opaque. I increased my visual sensor to adjust. Then we moved into a vein that made sucking noises. We slid along pretty fast and Mark telepathed to bear right at the next intersection. That vein was larger, so we began moving faster, and then Mark steered us through another small vein to the tumor. I recognized it from the pictures. We were touching the largest bulge of cancer cells. I could see the cells pulsing and one dividing. Mark had Valerie by his side. He gave her directions about what not to touch, but for the most part, there was little risk of that because the tumor was so big at this location. Valerie's AtCon started vibrating. Then she said, "Ready." Mark told her to engage the tissue. I watched carefully as Valerie held her position and cells started shrinking from the heat.

"Mark here. Move fourteen millimeters to the left. To the left again. How are you doing?"

"Valerie. Heat is steady still."

"Mark. Now come back to the right, but a little lower down. Good. Hold it there. To the right again and hold it."

"Valerie sending. My temperature is dropping to 50 degrees Celsius."

"Mark here. Just hold that position as long as you can. Fiona, you're in the box. Get your temp up to 60 degrees Celsius."

I started vibrating and realized that at this size, it is easier to generate heat. "Ready, Mark."

"Mark sending. Valerie, move to the back of the group and stand watch behind us. Fiona, take Valerie's position and engage the tissue next to where Valerie was working. Apply heat in that one spot."

I could see where cells were shrinking and looking damaged. I continued across the tumor with Mark timing me at each position. I finished the rest of the section of the tumor before I lost heat and felt fatigue setting in. I let Mark know.

"Mark here. Valerie and Fiona have treated the largest bulge on the tumor. Victor, follow me to the smaller bulge pressing against that artery."

I stood guard with Valerie while the men worked above us. My sensors were dimming. "Valerie, how are your visual sensors holding up?"

"They're dimming."

"Let's conserve what we can. You rest yours and we will use mine to scan the area. Fiona sending to Mark and Victor. We are conserving sensor power so light will dim now."

Mark was sending only to Victor, so we could not tell what was going on above us. My timer said that we had been working on the tumor for fifteen minutes. Now Victor was stepping back and Mark was working on the tumor. Another five minutes passed. Then three minutes. Finally I heard Mark say, "Everyone teleport out."

Back in Michael's room, Mark checked the monitors. "Blood pressure is elevated to normal and his heart is not working quite so hard. We took pressure off the ventricular artery. Until he regains consciousness, I can't tell about the paralysis on his left side, but his respiration is better. No indication here that we did him any harm, but we will know more about how much good we did in twenty-four hours."

"Victor here. What about his pain, Mark?"

"Mark here. Sorry Victor. I stayed away from the nerves this time. They are so small. I'm hoping that as the cells die and lose mass, more healthy tissues including nerves will be freed. I can then work around them. Success with our limitations means that we kill the entire tumor, but even so, we will leave scar tissue behind. Only a surgeon can cut that away and return his body to normal. Right now, I'm just trying to save his life. All we can do now is wait."

"Fiona here. While waiting, we need to replenish our energy. That means getting some sunlight and a good night's sleep tonight. Is there any reason that Valerie and I can't leave for a few hours?"

"Victor here. My wife is still sleeping. I would like Valerie to read her mind and let me know how she is, but my guess is that she will be around all the time."

"Valerie. Want to come with me?"

"Yes, Fiona. Can we see where the movie stars live? I saw a brochure with a map."

CHAPTER 16

The natural world is beautiful, whereas the world of particle physics is a claustrophobic surreal nightmare. Outside the hospital, the warm sun, bright colors, and soft breezes lifted our spirits and we wanted more. Valerie shared her memory of a brochure of movie stars' homes. The tour company was on Sunset Boulevard as well so we easily teleported to the address and hovered aboard one of the open-air vans. As we were motoring along, I was dumbstruck. I had never seen so many expensive cars—some I had never heard of before—so many beautiful gardens, and so many beautiful people. When we arrived in Beverly Hills, the driver's canned recitation about the homes of the celebrities was spell-binding. As we approached the home of Christina Aguilera, Valerie started bobbing up and down. "I have heard so much about her home in the magazines. She is my favorite celebrity! I would just die if I do not get to see her."

"Well in that case, let's go inside and take a look." I hovered out of the van and up the driveway to the front door with Valerie right behind me.

"Do we dare? Do we dare?"

"Why not? Didn't we just now save a young boy's life performing an excruciating bit of neurosurgery? We can do anything we want. I will give you my VIP tour of Christina Aguilera's home. Let's start with the grounds, gardens, and pool. I'm sure there is a pool around here somewhere."

We spent thirty minutes building up our energy stores while gasping at the swimming pool that looked like a river with boulders. Then we ventured into the palatial home. I liked the New Orleans style with the pink stucco and wrought-iron balconies, but the interior design was dominated by a shocking pink, red, and lavender color scheme. The red chandelier hanging over the red-carpeted curved staircase was too much like the stuff we'd seen inside Michael's veins.

Our tour peaked when we entered Miss Aguilera's dressing room, which was 120 square meters filled with clothes and a complete beauty parlor. I counted 254 pairs of shoes not including the ones scattered on the floor. But, alas, we caught no sight of the star herself.

It was nearing sunset when we hopped on a tour van going by and saw the rest of the neighborhood. Just before we teleported back to the room, Valerie whispered, "Being dead isn't all that bad."

Inside Michael's room, we found Victor's wife, Angelina, awake and talking to the doctor. I left Valerie to share Angelina's thoughts with Mark and Victor. It did not take a mind reader to see it was good news and those tears were tears of joy. I needed to scout for an empty room where I could spend the night. Michael's room was way too noisy and brightly lit for me to sleep well. When I returned, Angelina was gone and the AtCons were sharing information. Mark was sending. "Dr. Phelps is not the oncologist, but he is an internist who collaborates with oncologists in the care of cancer patients. His opinion is that Michael's vital signs are some improved and if he has a good night—meaning that there is no change in his vital signs—he will reduce his morphine and check his reflexes. I really don't want Michael to come off morphine before we kill the tumor. It is the only anesthesia option we have and it is critical that Michael be immobile. So I'm in a predicament."

"Fiona here. How long will it take us to kill the tumor? How much pain does our procedure generate for Michael? Is there another way we could assure that he is immobile?"

"Mark sending. I don't know how long it will take to kill the whole thing. If we leave any cells, it will come back, but we will be finished with the easy to reach stuff tomorrow. Then I can get by with just Valerie to help kill off the rest. You have a good point about the pain. If I can reduce pressure on the nerves, the pain is minimal. It is possible that I could work while he is sleeping, but if he moves at a critical time, I could kill healthy tissue."

"Fiona sending. Is there a way to reduce the cancer so that the doctors here could finish the job?"

"Mark sending. That is something to think about. They can do the same thing that I'm doing by injecting a needle into the tumor and sending an electrical current to kill cells. They can't see as well as I can, nor can they approach the tumor from as many different directions as I can. I can get behind the tumor—between it and some of the vessels and nerves. The ideal situation is for us to work as a team. Let them take care of what they can easily do in a well-lit operating theater while I work in the areas they can't reach. God, that would be exciting! I would be making history!"

"Fiona sending. Then let's work toward that end. Getting Michael well enough to undergo thermal ablation by the surgeons here. When they schedule him, then you can 'assist' without their awareness. That seems safer for you as well."

"Mark sending. Victor, are you OK with that? I can map out a strategy to do that and if it doesn't work, I can still proceed as we originally planned."

"Victor sending. Let's look at the pictures and see how that would affect what we do tomorrow. Yes, I agree in principle with Fiona's suggestion, but let's make sure we are thinking of everything so that tomorrow is productive."

"Fiona again. There's an empty room—928—down the hall. I'm bunking down there tonight. I need my beauty sleep if I'm going to be generating heat tomorrow. Any of you are welcome to join me, just be quiet and no lights."

"Wait for me, Fiona. I am exhausted from counting all those shoes and warding off some really creepy thoughts from some of the other tourists. What is butt fucking anyhow?"

CHAPTER 17

The next morning, I rejoined the others in Michael's room, feeling antsy about being away from the action back home. "Good morning. How is Michael?"

"Mark here. He had a good night. His vital signs are stable and we eavesdropped on Dr. Phelps' discussion with the nurse. They have taken him off hospice care for the moment, which means that the tumor is not in charge any longer. I'm going to take another look at it at noon, which will be twenty-four hours after our initial treatment. Then we will all go in for another assault on the tumor at 4:00 p.m. (PST). So be here and be rested. Until then, I only need Valerie to read minds."

So I found myself on my own in Los Angeles on a beautiful day, wondering if they had any other kind. Outside the hospital's main entrance was a huge eucalyptus tree that afforded a high perch. As I was thinking about which tour I might want to hitch a free ride on, I heard Mark sending a message. He was right below me.

"I'm up here, Mark."

"Oh, thank goodness I found you. I need your help. I promised Amelia that I would come to Denver and teleport with her to D.C. today."

"Does she realize that you can't actually teleport with another person?"

"No, she doesn't, but I think she would try it if someone was with her to reassure her and be there when the teleport ended."

"So as soon as you finish up here, you can go to Denver and do just that."

"I'm afraid that teleporting to Denver and then D.C. will be more than I can handle after an exhausting afternoon in surgery. And she is now in an empty house, which makes her anxious and depressed. She wants to be transported today."

"And since you are busy all day making medical history, you want me to do it and get back here by 4:00 p.m. (PST). Is that right?"

"Yes, could you please do this for me."

"You know what is worse than being an enabler, Mark? Enabling an enabler. But rather than cause you distress when you have so many more important things on your mind, I'm going to take care of your Amelia problem. Don't give it another thought. Give me the coordinates for the house in Denver and then the coordinates for the residence in D.C."

"Here they are."

"See you at 4:00 (PST) to help you with the assault. Bye."

I teleported to Denver and found myself inside a sleek, modern house with a view of the Rocky Mountains that might have been a postcard. I sent a telepathic message to Amelia and located her in the master bedroom.

"Fiona, friend of Mark, requests permission from Amelia to speak and be heard."

Amelia responded with, "Oh, don't be so formal. All this protocol is like we were a bunch of Star Wars freaks. It's enough that I'm frigging dead, do I have to also put up with . . . ."

"Shut the fuck up! As a dead self, you are about as functional as tits on a boar hog. What's worse, you're whiny, spoiled, and stupid. If you can't do for yourself, you can't do for your pod. Without a pod, you and Mark are on your own with no protection.

I am one of the people who must approve your admission to our pod. I WILL NOT ADMIT YOU TO OUR POD IF YOU CAN'T FOLLOW PROTOCOLS FOR TELEPATHIC MESSAGING AND TELEPORTING. So pay attention. I will give you instructions for telepath protocols. They will be stored in your memory. Follow them!

"Now, on the matter of teleporting, you can teleport anywhere that you can visualize or you can teleport to an address or set of coordinates. Coordinates are degrees of longitude, latitude and altitude. Don't forget altitude. Here are the coordinates for your D.C. destination."

"Now position yourself right in front of me. Note that I am rotating 10 degrees to the left and then 10 degrees to the right. This is a sign that I am very angry! Fix your attention on those coordinates that I just gave you. If you don't fucking disappear when I count to three, we will find out if you can die twice. One, two, . . . " Hmmm. I should have plenty of time to get back to LA and window-shop on Rodeo Drive.

When I rejoined the others, I was totally dumbfounded by all I had seen on Rodeo Drive. It was a world that I'd known existed, but had never seen. The mostly female shoppers looked like regular people—usual number of appendages and heads—so how could they afford those prices? I felt like a naïve, dumb hick. And some of that stuff looked just like something I might buy at Target. A plain sleeveless white shell was going for $120! I had forgotten about Amelia until Mark asked about her.

"Yes, Amelia in is D.C. now and she did it all on her own! It just took a woman's touch. While I was at it, I gave her the protocols for telepathic messaging. She wanted to learn them before she meets the rest of the pod. You can relax and lead this assault."

Since we all had been there, we simply teleported to the tumor site, which was a lot easier on Michael. Even I could tell the difference in the space around the brain stem from the first assault. Mark used us by turn to heat up various sections of cells that were most interfering with critical vessels and nerves. We were in there for thirty minutes and twenty seconds before Mark called it and we teleported back to the room.

"Mark sending. The cells we treated yesterday had diminished in size even since I checked them at noon. They are still dying, so it may be several days before we know how much good we have done. Now, we wait to see if there are any commensurate changes in Michael's condition. Dr. Phelps will check on him tonight and again in the morning. Valerie and I will hang around to collect that information. Thank you all for your help. You were cool, smart, and a well-coordinated team. If we do get a chance to work alongside living surgeons, I may call on you to assist."

"Fiona sending. Mark, if you don't need me, I'm heading home. Any messages for the rest of the pod from you guys?"

I duly recorded messages from Victor to the two Vinces and a message from Mark to Bennet. Valerie was being shy. So I said my goodbyes, teleported back to the library, and slept in my favorite dark corner of the microfiche archives.

CHAPTER 18

When I woke the next morning, Jonas was floating beside me. "It's been lonely around this place. Other than a couple of students hiding here to make out, the place has been deserted."

"Sorry I missed that. It has been too long for me as well. Anything new at the tobacco barn?"

"Nope. I think Demerson is a ghost in the past. But we have had some interesting discoveries out at the radio tower. Bennet shared some research from his memory store on the topic of physics and consciousness. Bennet's memory store is enormous, by the way. He must have every page of every Washington Post in there.

"Anyhow, apparently there has been very little research on the subject of human consciousness; there's not even an accepted definition of what it encompasses. Several serious scientists were discredited by earlier theories that were a tad quack-like, but as it turns out, they weren't so far off the mark. Their reputations were ruined and until the last twenty years, no one would go near the subject except to say that the brain played a role. But quantum mechanics changed all that. Mathematicians got into the act and started working on theories about how consciousness could be a thing or what Bennet calls 'a state of matter.' This one MIT physicist—Max Tegmark—outlined the basic properties a conscious system must have and, guess what? Those properties describe our AtCons. Bennet has nearly written a syllabus on the topic that confirms Tegmark's theories. And along the way Bennet has opened possibilities of other abilities that we may have—like telekinesis. He is on fire. Wants me to find a way that we can publish his paper that's in his memory store."

"Son of a gun! What a coup! If we can move things, we could operate computers!"

"Better, we already have computers or what Bennet calls a "computonium" in our AtCon that theoretically out performs today's computers by thirty-eight orders of magnitude. We just don't know how to activate it."

"Whoa. I thought my experience was mind-blowing, but this is even greater. Jonas, if we were a threat last week because we were asking questions, what are we now when we have answered those questions? My biggest news is that we dead selves successfully killed cancer cells. We interacted with the natural world and kicked butt! That is not supposed to be possible for AtCons.

"Jonas, I'm scared for us. Whoever has manipulated our afterlife cannot be pleased with the threat that we now pose. What would keep them from destroying us?

"If Victor's kid is better, then Victor needs to get back here. Tragic circumstances notwithstanding, we need his knowledge of how to manipulate radio waves to communicate with the AtCon originators before we lose our AtCons altogether. Maybe that is why we don't count as many dead selves as statistics would suggest."

"And then what, Fiona?"

"We negotiate. I'll go right now. We need everyone back here if it doesn't imperil the kid's life. Even if we just meet to compare notes. Then we can organize next steps based on what we collectively know."

"Fiona, how long will you be gone?"

I was at the hospital before I could even process his last utterance; anyhow, I had too much to do. As it turns out, Dr. Phelps was sufficiently puzzled over the improvement in Michael's reflexes that he called in the oncologist who did a new MRI. The shrinking of the tumor created quite a stir among the medical staff. No one had an explanation, but the doctors were ready to resume monitoring the tumor. In addition to the hard evidence, Valerie could now read Michael's mind. He was hungry and was remembering a baseball game with his father. His mother went home to rest, planning to have dinner with her son that evening.

Amidst all the jubilation, I got Mark and Victor off to the side to pass on the news from the radio tower.

"Mark sending. By all means, Victor is free to go. There will be at least a week of just letting Michael gain his strength and to gather more information on the tumor. Valerie and I will stay on top of things and she can come get you if and when we need you."

"Fiona sending. I really need all of you there today for a meeting, the purpose of which is to make decisions about assignments. This is a full pod meeting."

"Mark sending. I am a doctor, what value do I have in a discussion about AtCon computer capability or human consciousness and quantum mechanics?"

"Victor sending. Actually, that is what you have been doing these past few days, Mark. We have been applying quantum mechanics to affect change in cellular structures using high-frequency radio waves. I can see the value in your presence at the meeting."

"Fiona sending. Let's not waste time discussing this as if you have a choice. This is a pod meeting. Everyone must be there. Mark, leave now and collect Amelia. Be at the library at 8:00 p.m. (EST). Maybe you will get a chance to try piggyback teleporting. Victor, I would like for you to touch base with the Geeks Anonymous pod and Bennet at the radio tower ASAP. Get yourself up to speed and share what we did here so Bennet can be as informed as possible. We can't have a joint pod meeting of course, so it is important that we keep each pod informed by cross-training in related topics. Bennet is our linchpin with your pod. He will have to represent your pod at our meeting tonight. Go now. I will see to Valerie."

I left them and found Valerie. She read my thoughts before I could send. "You are upset with Mark. What did he do?"

"Mark doesn't take directions well. He wants to stay here with you to tend to Michael and I need him to get Amelia and be at a pod meeting tonight. You, too, of course. You will be seeing Bennet. That should be welcome news."

"Mark does not like Amelia. He likes me better."

"Don't tell me that you now have feelings for Mark."

"Okay, I will not tell you that."

"Mark is married, Valerie. He has responsibility for his wife. He is not free to have feelings for you."

"But you have feelings for Jonas and he is married to Israel."

"Marriage between the living ends with death, so, every dead self is unmarried. But there is a matter of personal responsibility as well. Jonas cannot be Israel's husband. They are forever lost to each other. But Mark is in an active, ongoing relationship with his wife. It is for Mark to end his relationship with Amelia before he assumes one with you. It's not ethical for him to deceive Amelia. It's called cheating in the natural world. Nor do you want to be involved with a man who is compromised in either his feelings or his obligations. That would limit how meaningful your relationship could be and puts you at risk of all sorts of ugly encounters with a pod mate, Amelia. For now, just work on being your best self and give Mark space to work things out.

"By the way, I can see why he would like you. You were outstanding during the tumor assaults. So brave and competent. I am proud of you, Valerie. Now let's go home. Race you!"

Back at the library an angry Mark was waiting for me. "Where is Amelia? She isn't at Kate's place and she isn't at our place in Denver."

"She has to be. I was standing in front of her at your house when she teleported. Show me the coordinates for Kate's place." I compared them with the coordinates he gave me and they were off slightly. I projected them back side-by-side.

"You gave me the wrong coordinates, Mark. Follow me and let's see if she's at the coordinates you telepathed to me."

The coordinates took me to the baggage claim area at Dulles Airport. What a frigging snafu! After the way I talked to that woman and I gave her the wrong coordinates! Mark was hovering beside me. "Okay Mark, you made a mistake but she should be here. You know her best. What would she do under the circumstances?"

"She's familiar with Dulles so she wouldn't be frightened. She knows that she is in D.C. She would wait for me to come get her."

"For how long? She arrived here about this time yesterday. Was there a place that she was accustomed to wait for you to pick her up?"

"No, she generally caught a taxi home. She hates waiting."

"What would she do if she couldn't catch a cab? There are no trains or buses out here are there?"

"No, but she would never take public transportation."

"With such bad results, would she dare try teleporting again?"

"Not likely, but I checked the house in Denver and she wasn't there."

"Well, this is my last idea other than patrolling the baggage claim area tonight after dark to see if we can spot her AtCon. She knows that she can teleport any place that she can visualize. Is there such a place here in D.C.?"

"We lived here for ten years. Our old house, our favorite restaurant?"

"What place would be the most comforting if she were afraid?"

"Amelia, wife of Mark Soren, sending to Fiona Campbell. Request permission to speak and be heard as pod mate."

"Fiona sending. Welcome. Speak and be heard."

"Amelia sending. I am so glad to have found you all. I've been looking everywhere. I teleported back-and-forth between here, Kate's place, Denver, and around the university library."

"Mark sending. Amelia, we just learned that the coordinates that Fiona gave you were off a little. I'm so sorry, dear."

"Amelia sending. Well, you know how I hate to wait and I was missing Samantha so much that I just figured out that I had Kate's address in my memory store so I teleported to that address and teleported to the other side of a couple of doors and into their apartment. Once I could visualize the building and the apartment, I went to find you and spied on some kids making out in the library.

Why didn't you tell me how much fun spying is? I can't wait to peek in on my old friends."

"Fiona sending. Amelia, congratulations on your resourcefulness. You will make a good pod mate. I will see you both at the pod meeting tonight at 8:00 p.m. (EST). Mark, make sure that Amelia gets there. We want to officially induct her into the pod."

CHAPTER 19

Jonas is the most powerful telepath in the pod, so he assumed responsibility for leading the meeting. Mark, Amelia, Bennet, Valerie, and I took positions around a study table with Jonas at the head. This gave us close proximity that made it easier to telepath to multiple receivers, but it also gave the affair a feeling of formality and order. Since Amelia did not know how to use a human voice yet, we sent thoughts rather than voice messages.

Jonas: Welcome, pod members, to our first meeting of six. Before we move to our agenda, I want to officially induct the new members. Inducted members Jonas Smith, Fiona Campbell, and Valerie Higgins have approved Bennet Soren, his son Mark Soren, and Mark's wife Amelia Soren for induction as full voting members of the Microfiche Pod. They are now voting members of the pod. Let's now recite our pledge as a group:

I, Jonas Smith, pledge my conscious resources to the protection and advancement of the Microfiche Pod. I place the welfare of the pod above my personal ambitions, my vanity, and material gain. I will conduct my personal affairs in a manner that brings respect and honor to the pod.

Let it be recorded that the pod membership is present and prepared to discuss and render opinions on the agenda items. Decisions are made through consensus with consensus defined as all members agreeing to a course of action. To facilitate discussion, I will resend comments to assure that all members receive each telepathic message. Bear with me if this bogs down.

Our first agenda item is a report on work to improve AtCon capacity submitted by Bennet.

Bennet: Some background first. The AtCon captures a dying person's consciousness—intelligence, personality, memories and identity—and shifts it from the locus of the human brain to an atomic configuration of multiple atoms—the AtCon. These are atoms within atoms that process, store and retrieve more efficiently than the brains of live selves. We theorize that at the point of death, the AtCon, which is a cloud of entangled atoms connected to the brain, starts sending signals by radio wave to a receiver in the ionosphere. Once free of the dead body, the AtCon is subject to settings that control—restrict or enhance—its capacities. The ones we most easily observe are our inability to telepath or otherwise communicate with more than a few dead selves at a time, our inability to interact with the natural world, and our inability to be seen or heard by live selves. We are effectively isolated to a few communicators. Since we can teleport with no difficulty and telepath within these limitations, we have to assume that there are reasons for these restrictions that are unrelated to our AtCon capacity.

Mark: What about my ability to kill cancer cells? Isn't that having an effect on the natural world?

Bennet: Victor briefed me on the tumor assaults. Brilliant work, son. Congratulations to you and your entire team. However, it makes my point. Your effect was at the cellular level where the natural world is governed by particle physics rather than

Newtonian physics. Continuing my report, our work at the radio tower establishes that there is a force that controls our AtCons. This force has access to our AtCons and regularly reviews our memory stores. We are reasonably sure that the connection is a form of radio wave compatible with the radio waves that we use in sending telepathic messages. And that it is also compatible to a pulsar that American astronomers have been monitoring for the past seven years, ten months, three weeks, and four days. This was determined by comparing the dispersion measures—DMs—of the two waves. This suggests that the originators are highly sophisticated in satellite technology or even may be from another planet.

Bennet paused to let this last statement sink in. Then he resumed.

With Victor back, we are well positioned to send a message from multiple AtCons at a higher frequency but still with the same DM that may find the receiver. It may be possible to make contact with the entities who control our afterlife.

We also found a way to use our AtCons to communicate with each other simultaneously using a different radio frequency that no one outside the pod can access. Right now it functions like the old-fashioned telephone party lines. Each of us will be on the same wavelength so a message to one will be picked up by all six of us. Telepath protocols can be adjusted so that the intended receiver can be identified, but there is no privacy to this process. And because the radio waves are low-frequency at the moment, it takes time for them to travel distances. Eventually we should be able to improve the service. Once this is instituted, we can communicate to everyone with the correct settings and a Morse code translator in their memory store. Report concluded.

Jonas: Bennet is now projecting the complete, more detailed version of his report for your memory store. Now you can review it and comment.

Fiona: Are the Geeks Anonymous planning to make contact with the originators? Also, when will our intercommunication system be ready for us to use? And what is involved in its implementation?

Bennet: The Geeks are not prepared to make contact with the originators until after they have an independent communications system set up that includes access to the Internet. They are creating radio interference at night when their AtCons are at rest to protect the privacy of their memory stores. With Victor back, we should be able to start installing a setting in your AtCons in a week. Allow another week to work out kinks.

Jonas: Does this new communication system allow us to telepath to everyone on the radio wave simultaneously, i.e., if we had it today, your report would not have to be forwarded by a facilitator to each listener, right?

Bennet: Yes, you are right. Which is why it is critical to have it in place before we engage the originators. Our security will depend on our ability to coordinate and share information in real time.

Jonas: With the communication barrier out of the way, do we want to expand our pod to include the Geeks Anonymous? Or is there another way we can include them for certain communications?

Bennet: There is a way we can have separate internal communications and still share a third one. It would involve installing settings for two radio frequencies plus the one we already have. I can't say what issues that may raise, but I can get an answer. My suggestion is that we now function as separate teams with me as the link between the two. I will filter all information going from one pod to the other.

Fiona: Combining pods is more than just working together on one project; we have to share the same mission. With the pod's approval, I will study the matter, confer with Geeks Anonymous about their wishes and technical issues, and report back to you.

Amelia: It seems that we are getting all excited about talking to one another and ignoring the horrible possibility that we are about to aggravate someone who can destroy us. Wouldn't it be better to disconnect their radio wave and make ourselves hard to find rather than knocking on some alien's door?

Jonas: We don't know that we are dealing with aliens. We could be dealing with dead scientists who have amassed the expertise to assume control over the consciousness of dead people through their AtCons.

Valerie: Either way, if the originators of our AtCons are evil, we would have seen evidence of this by now.

Jonas: Bennet, would you make a recommendation based on your informed judgment about the proposal to implement the radio-wave-communication plan to members of this pod?

Bennet: Yes, I so move.

Jonas: All in favor send an affirmative message. I count six affirmatives. That motion is carried. Valerie, will you meet with Bennet and take responsibility for getting pod members to the radio tower at a time convenient to Geeks Anonymous? Fiona, please follow up with a report supporting your recommendation about merging the two pods five days from this hour.
Does anyone want further discussion regarding making contact with the entities that are controlling our AtCons? After ten minutes and twenty-two seconds, I hear no one wanting further discussion. Does anyone wish to make a recommendation on this matter?
Amelia: Recommend that we sever or disconnect our AtCons from the radio wave link to the originators and relocate our pod away from this area.

Jonas: All in favor of Amelia's proposal, send an affirmation message. After ten minutes and twenty seconds, there is only one affirmation. We do not have consensus. Is there anyone wanting to make a different recommendation on this matter?

Bennet: I recommend that we develop a strategy for how we may respond should our efforts to make contact succeed. What do we want to convey in our initial message, what would be our back-up position if we get a hostile response, who should our spokesperson be, and so forth. I don't think we are ready to move forward at this time, but I am in favor of a plan for resolving this one way or the other. We can't have this specter over our heads. We need to know what we are up against.

Jonas: Any further discussion or other points? After ten minutes and thirty-three seconds, discussion is closed. Those who are in favor of Bennet's recommendation send an affirmative message. There are five affirmations. We don't have consensus. Amelia does not approve.
Is there any other business before the pod?

Mark: What about our assignments? Fiona made a big deal that we would learn what next steps there would be. And we're at a stalemate. It seems that there was not enough preparation made to assure a productive meeting. I left a dying child to be here and I don't intend to jump at the pod's command if this is all that we accomplish.

Jonas: Mark, your assignment is to be fitted first with the new intercommunication settings. While you are waiting, meet with Bennet and Victor to see if you can further develop their theories about consciousness and its relationship to quantum mechanics. Your experience and knowledge of nanotechnology and neuroscience would be useful. While you're tending to that, Valerie will return to the hospital and monitor Michael's condition; she will return if there is any unexpected change. Bennet will provide reading resources for you.

Mark: I respectfully decline my assignment.

Jonas: On what basis?

Mark: I have more important work to do that also calls for my medical background.

Jonas: Your first priority is to the pod, not to a patient, even one who is related to a friend. Are you saying that you are unwilling to honor your pledge? If so, then you must leave the sanctuary of the pod.

Amelia: My God, Mark, stop being such an asshole. Just because you are a doctor, you don't get to put your work ahead of everything else and strut around like king of the hill. You got by with that with me, overriding my plans at the last minute with some excuse about work. Life and death, you would say, but then I find out that you were playing golf. Well, this is a new ball game and I'm not one of your fans, so I vote that you do what you are told.

Jonas: Mark, what is your decision?

Mark: Of course it if is really important, I will stay as long as it takes.

Jonas: Any other business? Having waited ten minutes and fifteen seconds with no other business brought before the pod council, I conclude the meeting.

Jonas looked tired. "The hour is late. Valerie and Bennet will give Mark and Amelia a tour of our pod headquarters where you are welcome to spend the night, any night. Valerie, will you repeat the message from your location as well?"

I moved close to Jonas who was giving off that blue-gray storm cloud aura. "Shall we review the meeting events?"

"I really liked my life much better when I was not part of a pod. Tell me again why we formed the pod?" Jonas asked in a muted voice.

"To protect and develop Valerie."

"And this is served by adding Mark in what way?"

"She needs close exposure to men, to learn about them. She led the life of a teenage recluse before she died. The same can be said of you. It's about learning social skills."

"Which I only need if I want to socialize. Here is what happens. You will create relationships with dead selves who will disappoint you—betray you even—and eventually disappear. Even in death, permanence is not guaranteed in the relationship department." Jonas sounded exasperated.

"Then she needs to learn that and not take it personally. She needs to have the internal resources that are strong and secure so she only has to depend on herself, so she won't be needy and vulnerable to others. My brief experience as a dead self is that the deceased are flawed in much the same way as the living are. Death does not change who we are. So suck it up and make the best of the situation. She needs behavioral options. The pod is a learning laboratory for her. And maybe for the rest of us as well.

"Something you should know, Jonas. Case in point. Mark is a jerk. He gave me the wrong coordinates and sent me to Amelia to convince her to teleport by teleporting with her. I gave her a hard time and told her she had to do this by herself. And she did. And ended up at Dulles Airport rather than Kate's place. That mistake was either a deliberate attempt to keep me out of the way for a while, or it was a major Freudian slip. And then when we found her, he implied it was my error."

"Why would he want you out of the way in Los Angeles?" Jonas' AtCon was resuming its normal blue color.

"For the same reason he bucked your directions at the meeting tonight. He resents being subject to our authority. Also, he is hitting on Valerie and wants time alone with her. I already talked to her. She understands the complications that can develop around a cheating man. It will be interesting to find out what Valerie learns from our pod members as she escorts them on the tour, but I hope she at least sees his true self."

"What does she say about my true self?" Jonas' question surprised me.

"She has shared nothing with me. When I learned she could read minds, I asked her to keep such information confidential and she agreed. I presume she gives you the same courtesy and respect."

"What do you want to do at this point to resolve this?" Jonas asked.

"Be patient. The best possible outcome is that Valerie works this out on her own."

"Fine, just as long as she doesn't start crying again. I hate that."

NOW THAT I'M DEAD

CHAPTER 20

The expansion of the Microfiche Pod seemed to have a soothing effect on both pods. There was a formal order, protocols to follow for communications and decision making, and an informal hierarchy. To some small extent at least, our pods' members had some structure that lessened the uncertainty of an open organization. Consequently, our work groups were becoming more productive. Jonas took an interest in the Geeks Anonymous work and was slowly building technical skills that were useful even though his primary job was Vince Senior's handler. With Jonas around, Vince Senior was calmer and more cooperative with Vince Junior, Victor, and Bennet. After a lot of deliberation, we shared our ability to telepath voice messages. Vince Senior belittled the whole idea since the use of a speaking voice has no effect on their communication system, which sent information like an e-mail that you could read in your head. But the rest of the geeks took to it.

An added bonus of the pods' collaboration was that Jonas and Bennet were developing a strong bond of mutual respect. Bennet was the "adult" in the group who demonstrated a calm demeanor at all times, facilitated good communications among the workers, and was a good teacher of applied physics. His knowledge was shared with the group while the geeks had difficulty conveying their cyber skills to Bennet. Or else Bennet had no affinity for computers.

Meanwhile, Valerie was at the hospital collecting information on Michael and watching non-stop American television. Although Michael got to choose the stations, mostly sports channels and TMZ, there were times that Valerie was able to sample news and talk shows before he changed channels. She was there for two weeks and let us know at her last visit that she was ready to move on to something more substantive.

Once Mark's AtCon setting was adjusted to send and receive at the new radio wave frequency, he was used to test the strength and length of time communications took. For purposes of back and forth conversations, the frequency worked well for dead selves within a mile of each other. Longer distances led to forced pauses that made conversation awkward, but reliably sent messages that could be received eventually. We were now gathered to see how it worked across the country. Mark had teleported back to the hospital to relieve Valerie and we were waiting for his message to arrive. He was to send at 2:00 p.m. (EST) and it was now that time.

After thirty minutes with nothing, Amelia offered her assessment, "I bet he totally forgot. I remember when he forgot our tenth wedding anniversary dinner party. He was preoccupied with a patient's test results. Right now, I bet he's totally focused on Michael."

Another thirty minutes passed and Valerie appeared. "I thought I should let you know that Mark is busy catching up on Michael's medical records. He said he would call tomorrow at the same time. I knew you might worry and teleported to assure you that nothing was wrong."

"How is Mark able to peruse the electronic records?" Jonas asked.

"The last shift change in nurses was interrupted during an entry and the file was never closed. That happens a lot. If I crank up my send-wave frequency like we did when we were creating heat for the thermal ablation assault, it causes the computer to scroll up and down within the file. I showed Mark how to do it. It's hard to learn to control the computer that way, but with practice, I was able to go back to the last entry. I read the files left open and sent him copies of everything in my memory store. He is going over those now."

"Fiona here. It's good to have you back. Bennet, would you please get Valerie over to the radio tower and let the geeks debrief her so you can put her to work. She has a lot of computer savvy to offer. Valerie, darling, let's catch up tonight. Welcome home."

"Well, we will try again tomorrow and I will assure you that Mark will send at the appointed time. I appreciate your patience." Jonas had an edge to his voice.

Jonas came close. "Fiona. Where is everyone?"

"Valerie received the radio tower coordinates from Bennet and the two disappeared. Amelia returned to Kate's apartment since Samantha would be home from school soon. It worries me that I still haven't found a really good spot in the pod for Amelia's abilities. She is getting bored. That's never a good situation."

"Worry about that later. Right now I propose that you and I pay Mark a visit. Is there a way to do that and no one be the wiser?"

"That depends on the timing. After 2:00 p.m. (EST) tomorrow we could go. This is about Mark? I'm troubled by his passive aggressive behavior as well, but we cannot risk alienating him. We have no power over him other than to kick him out of the pod; and as satisfying as that may be, it would also be a loss. What pod has its own medical doctor? And right now, he and Victor are the only ones who are equipped to send on the new radio-wave frequency."

"The test could go through without us here since Victor is the only one who can receive right now. What if we let both pods know that we are teleporting out now to make sure that Mark does what he is supposed to do? Everyone should meet at the radio tower to note the results of our beta test. That would send the message that insubordination will not be tolerated while our actions with Mark will not be observable."

"And just what are our actions with Mark?"

"I'm working on that, but I won't do anything without your approval, promise. Also, since I have you alone, I should let you know that on one of Valerie's trips back she asked me for pictures of vaginas."

"She asked what?"

"Vaginas. She cannot find a picture of one in any of the books she has consulted and she needs that in order to have an anatomically correct hologram. She reminded me that since she was born a male and had never had sex with a girl, she never saw one. The medical books provide drawings, but no actual pictures that she can copy."

"And why would she ask you and not me, since I obviously have one."

"Her assumption is that I have seen more lady parts than you have, and can give her a selection from which to choose, like the way she chooses from different clothes styles.

"Fiona. I can hear you laughing."

"Of course I'm laughing. We forget how smart she is. She reasoned all this out quite logically. And she's right. You probably have seen a lot of vaginas in your day, whereas I have only seen the one."

"What should I do?"

"Send her pictures of your most attractive vagina memories, something age- and size-appropriate."

"But then she can have sexual intercourse."

"Yes and I hope she will enjoy it. Relax, I will give her the talk, but she's ready and it's natural for her to experiment with men and sex. At least we know there will be no unwanted pregnancies, STDs, or injury."

"Do you think that the two pods comprise the entire pool of possible mates? Could she have met another AtCon in California?"

"If she did, she would tell us. At least she would not lie to us about it. OK, I will add that to my talk. Which I want to do before we leave, so when do you want to take off?"

"Tonight at 7:00 p.m. (EST). Meet me here and we will teleport at the same time."

"And what do we do between then and 2:00 p.m. (PST) tomorrow?"

"Sightsee. Have some fun. It will be 4:00 p.m. (PST) and I would make a good travel guide. Meanwhile, talk to Valerie and I will send her pictures of vaginas."

"You also need to let all the guys know that a single virgin is coming of age and we expect them to show her the utmost respect. And, Jonas, it wouldn't hurt if you presented us as her protectors so they know who they would have to deal with."

"Good point. Most of these men are terrified of you."

NOW THAT I'M DEAD

CHAPTER 21

I caught up with Valerie when she returned from the radio tower at 5:03 p.m. (EST). She was in her favorite hiding place, on the last empty shelf in the bound periodicals section. She hardly noticed my approach. "Hey. What're you up to?"

"Oh, I am looking at vaginas that Jonas sent me."

"Do you see anything you like?"

"Can I change the color of the pubic hair if I want to?"

"If Jonas can change the color of his eyes, I don't see why you couldn't change the color of pubic hair."

"Well, they all look much alike. One seems to be pretty sturdy and plump, but is blond. The other one that I like is very petite with very little hair that is black and matches the rest of my hair. What do you think?"

"With your build, it seems that the petite one would be more compatible. But you can always change out if you aren't happy."

"No, I fail to express myself well. What do you think my partner might like?"

"Oh. I have never known a man to complain or really care. Just pick one and see how it feels to both you and your partner. Then refine your search based on the feedback."

"Excellent solution. I knew you would know what to do, Fiona."

"Since we are on that subject, are you planning to have sex soon?"

"No, I just want to be ready so I can be spontaneous. Jonas says it is best to plan well if you want to be spontaneous."

"So there's no one special that you're considering?"

"You are thinking about Mark, are you not? Amelia is right about one thing. Mark is a wanker. Wankers are a total turn off. Besides, I am too young for Mark. I noticed on TMZ that the guys I find attractive are more muscular and nimble. They can do these great dance moves."

"You know that TV performers aren't like real people, don't you?"

"Of course, but they make good templates for AtCon holograms. I could not see Mark ever creating a young AtCon hologram. He thinks he is perfect as he is."

"Okay. Well, if you have any questions about the act of intercourse, just let me know. I have no experience with sex as a hologram-inspired memory myself, but at least I have memories of sexual orgasms to draw on. I recall that you have never had sex either as a boy or girl."

"But I had sex with myself as a boy and, you forget. I can read minds, so I can share other people's memories."

"And the most important aspect of sexual gratification is to be uninhibited. You have that in spades as well. So, you are all set, it seems.

"By the way, I'm going to visit Mark at the hospital later tonight. Jonas and I will be with him tomorrow to make sure that the test goes off okay. Is there anything I should know about the two pods before I take off and you can't reach me?"

"You mean what did I hear during the tour? Just the usual complaints from Mark. He had a fleeting thought of finding another pod. Amelia on the other hand, really, really dislikes him. She thinks he caused the accident that killed them. He was scolding her as she was driving and grabbed the steering wheel when he thought she had missed their exit. The car crashed into an abutment."

"Fucking unbelievable! You just never know to look at them that he is the freak in the marriage.

"We need to find a way to keep Amelia busy and the good doctor occupied but not in the same place. Any ideas?"

"Amelia likes you a lot. Maybe working with you on something. Oh. I wish to thank you for assigning me to the radio tower. Being over there is different with Bennet and Jonas in the group. Once I catch up with the rest, I think I am really going to be excited about the work."

"You're welcome, hon. Keep thinking about Amelia and we will talk when I get back."

I found Jonas alone in the study. "Are you ready to take off?" I asked.

"Yeah. Let's get out of here. Flash me the coordinates for the hospital."

The next minute, we were in Michael's room, but it was empty. The bed was unmade. "They must have moved Michael since his condition improved. He's probably in pediatrics. There's a directory by the elevator." I teleported and returned. "Pediatrics is on the third floor, two floors down. Let's hover down the stairs."

As we neared the exit for the third floor, Jonas and I simultaneously picked up a telepath message and stopped quickly. Were there other dead selves in the hospital? It wouldn't be unheard of. We listened.

"I have a good mind to not show up tomorrow as well, just to make my point. I don't take orders from some backwoods slave from the nineteenth century. Of course, you are right Victor. Now is not the time to rock the boat. I know I can bring Amelia—for whatever that's worth—and Dad. Blood is thicker than water among us Jews. I may be able to bring Valerie. She has a crush on me. That would give us a pod with real clout. Okay. I'll play nice for now and do the demonstration of our new radio wave frequency tomorrow. I'll update you on Michael then as well. Bye."

We retraced our path back to the fifth floor, far enough that our telepaths would not be accidentally picked up. Jonas was furious. "That shithead! He will long regret this stunt."

"First things first. Let's find a safe place to talk and think this through."

"Here are some coordinates. Meet me there."

The coordinates took me to a house overlooking the ocean. It was luxurious with a large redwood deck, fireplaces inside and on the deck. Stairs connected the house to the beach below. Jonas seemed to know his way around. We teleported to the other side of the door. The place was empty.

Jonas needed to vent. "That was a conversation between Mark and Victor, which must be on the new radio wave line that they've been using to plot against our pod. I never thought Victor would stoop so low, although he was the one who killed Valerie by using her brain as a transmitter."

"I agree. I didn't see that coming. If anyone, I would have suspected Vince Senior. But they must all be in on it, since each of the geeks has stonewalled me when I've tried to talk about combining the pods."

"They would have to be."

"Even Bennet?"

"Maybe not Bennet. He was more invested in the question of identity of the force behind the AtCons. What about Valerie?"

"Definitely not Valerie. I talked to her just before I left. She is totally turned off by Mark and now looking for a younger man like the ones she saw on TMZ. "

"But why didn't she pick up on his thoughts? He must have leaked his thoughts at some unguarded moment."

"He did. She told me that during the tour she read a thought about leaving the pod, but nothing more. Remember that they have not been together for the last two weeks, except when Mark returned day before yesterday. If he concentrated on medical records the whole time she was here, then she would not have known. We can conclude then that this insurrection has come up since the surgery."

"What would we do if we lost everyone?" Jonas' AtCon had taken on his storm cloud coloration.

"I thought you didn't like being part of a pod? It infringed on your freedom and carefree lifestyle."

"You knew I was lying, didn't you?"

"Oh, yeah. I like being part of a pod as well. It's like a family that we made so that we could have a family to love. A worst-case scenario is that the pod will be reduced to the three of us—you, me, and Valerie. That is where we started, not so long ago."

"I'm feeling better already."

"Then add this to your happy pile. If we do have a hostile force out there, its links are with the other pod, not us. True, our memory store will show some culpability, but the Geeks Anonymous pod is where the rubber hit the road. If there is any retaliation, the 'originators' will take out the communication system and the AtCons who engineered it."

"You have a phenomenal ability to analyze information and come to logical conclusions."

"It's a knack I have. I was tested by the Defense Department before they would give me a top security clearance. They wanted to know more about my abilities to make sure I was not spying— their first thought when I came up with solutions or conclusions that were classified. Turns out that I test at the 98th percentile on that one trait. I was promoted to an SES position—Senior Executive Service."

"But you said you were a GS-15; isn't that lower?"

"I was demoted when my analytical skills turned up anomalies in defense procurements. I blew the whistle and was summarily demoted. Then, they put me on a research detail that is nothing more than a turkey farm for GS misfits of high rank, most of whom are idiots with impressive degrees. With a meager BA in public administration, I was shunned on study projects, treated like the unwashed heathen. Ironic isn't it that the two things that meant the most to me—my education and my two daughters—brought me no real joy. I died a woman who no one really cared about or would remember."

"I'll never forget you. For whatever it is worth, you have my love and respect."

"Believing you fills me with joy—joy that I inspire such feelings and joy that I can return them. Jennifer is the only other person to leave me feeling cherished and unafraid to love in return.

"Who's Jennifer?"

"A lovely lady from my youth who gave me my one big break, but that's a story for another time. What should we do about what we learned?"

"Nothing right now. Their not knowing that we are on to them is a tactical advantage. Let's play it straight tomorrow and then head home and make sure that you and I are the next ones wired up for long-distance telepathy. We can then eavesdrop on their calls. Let's explore the matter with Valerie as a what-if scenario, but not reveal what we know. Valerie is likely to spill the beans out of naiveté born of virtue."

"I know what you mean. Which of us is closer to Bennet?"

"He likes us both, but he is bound to trust you the most since you were alive together. I have to ask, was there anything romantic between you two?"

"No. Nothing. We were friends at Potomac Gardens—two of the few people with brains and a shared value system. And to answer the unasked question, I don't 'fancy' him either."

"So, do I have a chance to be more than a loving friend?" Jonas' AtCon had assumed its soft coral pink.

"Are you ready to accept someone in Israel's place?"

"I think so. I have to be honest with you. I will never stop loving her, but I also want to be loved by you. Is it enough that I will be totally devoted to you and your happiness?"

"It is more than I ever thought I would have, but I have to warn you, Jonas. I have never been able to pull off a lasting relationship with a man. Either I get tired of him or he betrays my trust, usually over another woman. Also, I don't like being bossed around."

"Who doesn't know that? Well, we have some work ahead of us if we try. At least we have our feelings out in the open. Whew! I've been trying to do that for months now. I am willing to celebrate that much. Let's don our holograms and watch the sunset on the deck like we own the place."

Jonas reverted to the California style of soft flannel slacks and a knit, short-sleeved shirt with a sports coat. That man must spend hours poring through GQ.

I remembered an outfit in Valerie's collection—long flowing skirt of sienna-colored, textured raw silk, with a simple white silk shirt and wide leather belt and silver sandals. My hair and makeup was perfect. Yes, I had planned so I could be spontaneous.

We took each other in and smiled. He reached out his hand and I stepped forward slowly and clasped it to the sound of "When a Man Loves a Woman." He could telepath music! We danced slowly as I built up skill and confidence with hologram motion. Another song followed. "Let's Be Together." The sun set into the mist of the fog coming in. The temperature dropped and the gas fireplace in the living room, set to a thermostat, started up. Inside, standing by the fire, I could imagine its warmth as I could feel the warmth of the man holding me. Jonas whispered, "Remember the dinner we shared at the club? Remember the last time you stood this way with someone?"

I recalled not one particular man, but all the good men in my life: the ones who loved me and enjoyed my body as I enjoyed theirs. I projected those remembered moments on this man, this moment. I could feel the contours of Jonas' muscles under the fabric of his jacket and pants. I imagined his jacket off and it disappeared. He grinned and my skirt and belt disappeared. I stood there in bikini lace panties, silver sandals, and white blouse, shirttails falling to my hips. I removed his knit shirt and ran my hands over his chest and arms. With my face against his chest, his arms tightened around me and pulled me close to him. I raised my face for a kiss and as our tongues caressed and our lips worked their magic, all our clothes disappeared. We were naked and touching. My remembered pulse was pounding in my ears as he picked me up and carried me to the bedroom and laid me down in one long, slow, fluid motion without breaking contact with my skin. We kissed. He looked deep in my eyes and said, "What do you like?"

"No talking. Touch me. Everywhere."

And he did. I had tried to imagine making love to Jonas in hologram form, but I could never quite do it. Now? I can't imagine making love any other way. The possibilities for sexual stimulation are limitless. Your partner can be everywhere at once. Gravity can be employed to enhance the memory of basic sex endlessly. And Jonas was an experienced master of hologram motion.

We slept five hours, forty minutes, and twenty-three seconds. The rest of the time we made love. It was now 8:00 a.m. (PST). We needed to be at the hospital for the beta test at 11:00 a.m. (PST). I wanted to luxuriate in the afterglow, that wondrous "in love" feeling where we exchange tender glances. But Jonas was sleeping soundly in the bed that was not even slightly mussed.

I dressed in a pair of white linen slacks, tissue-thin cotton top, an open-weave grey poncho, and the same silver sandals. Jonas found me sitting on the deck, basking in the sun and beauty of a classic southern California day. The blue Pacific pounded the beach and several surfers in black wetsuits were on boards. To think that people can start their days like this all the time. Does it get boring?

"Not if you stop and have sex every so often." Jonas came up behind me, kissed my neck, and sat in the chaise next to mine. "Did I mention at any time last night that I loved you? The events started blurring together so that I had a hard time distinguishing my body from yours and whose message I was picking up—yours or mine."

"Well to set the record straight, I was chanting 'I love you' like a mantra. And I can say it again here in the clear light of day. I love you, cowboy."

"In the same spirit: I love you, Fiona. And sex with you is like something from a dream. Not that it matters, but do you think we can keep this a secret once we are home?"

"Certainly not from Valerie. Is there some reason why we should?"

"I don't know. I'm just feeling paranoid as hell. Could someone . . . would someone use our feelings for each other to some advantage?"

"We can keep it quiet for now, but my guess is that people we are close to will pick up on our feelings, particularly Valerie. If you are paranoid, a better plan may be to figure out who might take advantage of your feelings for me. Who do you suspect?"

"You're right. I'm just overreacting to Mark's betrayal."

We sat holding hands, drawing energy from the sun. I told him about Jennifer rescuing me from an abusive father, but did not get into details about the nature of the abuse. He was appropriately sympathetic and did not pry. But when I came to the part where Jennifer moved away without me, he blinked his eyes and looked off into the distance. His sadness showed in the slump of his shoulders and the set of his jaw. I felt a wave of tenderness for this man who had suffered so much and still felt his loss. His rabbit hole must be is as deep and twisted as mine. I squeezed his hand and changed the subject.

"It would not do if we were late to Mark's gotcha party and we need some extra time to locate Michael's room.

We teleported in our AtCons back to the hospital.

NOW THAT I'M DEAD

CHAPTER 22

At the hospital, I found Michael's room number from the receptionist's patient finder screen and we teleported there. It was 10:44 a.m. (PST) and Mark was expecting us. "I take it that you are here to chastise me for missing my appointment yesterday."

Jonas took the lead. "No. We'd just have to listen to your bullshit story if we did that. I am simply here to see what goes on in a hospital room. I died before any such service was available, so this is the only time I have ever been inside a hospital. Tell me what all that equipment does."

Mark explained how the monitors worked and showed us the MRIs recently taken and still posted on the viewer on the wall. "As you can see by this film, the tumor is half the size it was before I used thermal ablation to kill cells. This reduction in mass has restored a lot of Michael's normal function. He is at physical therapy right now, but his quality of life is already much improved."

"Can the remaining tumor continue to grow?" Jonas asked.

"Yes, unless it's all killed, it will come back. That is why they are planning another thermal ablation using needles and a small camera. My work freed enough space for them to get to all the tumor now."

"So why are you needed at this point?" sent Jonas.

"I can still reach areas that they are likely to miss. See this section between the spinal cord and the artery? My AtCon can reach that and kill those cells. And these over here that are growing around this nerve. I have far greater accuracy than they will have. I can get every cell in that area, one cell at a time if necessary."

"Very impressive. I can see why you are Victor's new best friend." Jonas moved away from the viewers. "Now it is time to make the test call. Have you been practicing the protocols?"

"Nothing to it. Just have to concentrate on the setting codes and send as I would a normal telepath. Here goes."

A minute passed, then Mark's message came through. "Mark sending to Victor." Another minute passed. "Yes, I read you, Victor. Fiona and Jonas are here. How do you want to proceed with the test? All right, I will repeat your message when you say 'three.' It is time for all good men to come to the aid of their country." There was a pause while Mark waited for Victor. "Again? It is time for all good men to come to the aid of their country. Anything else?" Another pause.

"Okay. I will pass on the message. Mark over and out."

"Victor said that the test is a success and that it takes two minutes for our sent messages to reach the other coast. He thinks he can speed that up and wants to hold off installing the settings to other pod members until then."

"I see. That is great news! Well, Fiona and I have some other business in the area, so we will leave you to your doctoring. Sorry I missed seeing Michael. Ciao."

Jonas and I teleported to the library immediately where we almost landed on Amelia. "Amelia, why aren't you at the radio tower witnessing the beta test of the new radio wave?"

"Those men are so rude to me. I'm sure that Mark has turned them against me. I don't go there unless Valerie or Bennet is around. Did the test go well? Can I go in and get set up to use it tomorrow?"

"Victor wants to do some tweaking before installing it, so when we know, you'll know. But I promise you it won't be long. Can you tell me where Bennet is?" Jonas asked.

"I can't find either of them. Valerie was supposed to give me a holograph lesson this afternoon, but it's time now for me to get home to Samantha. Tell her that I will try to get in early in the morning for a session. I can't wait to wear clothes again."

Amelia disappeared. Clearly she was not involved in the geek rebellion.

"You have any idea where Valerie might be hiding out?" Jonas was checking high and low around the study. The problem with AtCons is that they can shrink to next to nothing if someone wants some privacy.

"Is there any place in the library where a couple could go to have hologram sex at this time of day? I mean Valerie and Bennet, not us."

"Follow me."

He led me to an equipment closet on the top floor of the library. We teleported to the other side of the door and what we saw caused us to teleport back. Valerie and Bennet were in flagrante. Bennet in his young man hologram was naked and leaning across an equally naked Valerie with a perfect vagina presented.

"Do you think they saw us?" I was sending with 25 percent force.

Jonas moved further away and whispered, "I doubt it. They were pretty focused."

"What should we do?"

"Stay nearby and wait for them to come out."

"Based on our most recent experience, that could take all day."

"Or longer. The equipment closet has a lot of loose electrons in it."

"Let's give them an hour and then you can summon them."

We returned to the study.

Jonas said, "We need to get those new settings installed. Do you think Valerie or Bennet would know how?"

"Valerie may if she was around when they were installing settings for Mark or one of the others. Probably all of the geeks have access to the link by now. But remember what Amelia said. Are we overly concerned about communications when the main thing is making contact with the 'originators'? Of course that would require Bennet's help. Let's face it. We can't do much of anything without at least one of them. How long has it been?"

"About half an hour or so. Say have you noticed that we have been using vague imprecise measurements? Jesus. We have to get them. It's starting! Our AtCons are breaking down!" I instantly registered the fear in his voice.

We raced to the equipment closet and Jonas called them. And called them again. Finally we teleported to the other side of the door. They were in a stupor in their AtCon form. "Jonas, we have to get them out of here. What can we do?"

"Vibrate your AtCon against Valerie. I'm doing the same for Bennet. Maybe the vibration will act as a reset button."

We did that for a while and Valerie's AtCon started humming louder. "Valerie. You have to get out of here. Teleport to the study NOW!" She disappeared. I turned my attention to Bennet's AtCon. Jonas was running out of steam. I joined him and vibrated against Bennet on the other side. We heard a soft hum that grew louder. His AtCon was starting to right itself. "Bennet, you have to teleport to the study. Teleport Bennet. Get out of here!! Get out now!!" He disappeared. Jonas telepathed me, "You first." I teleported to the other side of the door. "I'm by the door. Come to me, Jonas."

His AtCon appeared beside me. I started laughing, probably a state of hysteria. I felt so light, I just wanted to float in the air. "Jonas, my love. We are on the right side of the door. Let's get to the light at those windows." He floated erratically behind me until we made it to the windowsill. I gazed at the top of a maple tree below me. The green was startling, like I had never seen green before.

I kept my AtCon touching Jonas' AtCon, so he could perhaps draw energy from me. I wish to hell I understood better how all this worked. After a short time, he telepathed. "I feel very strange."

"Jonas, can you make it down to the study? We need to check on Valerie and Bennet."

"No, let me stay longer by the window. Catch up later."

"Jonas, don't try to teleport. Just hover down, window by window when you can. I'll check on you in ten minutes."

I teleported to the study. Valerie and Bennet were there on Jonas' sofa. There were no windows in this section of the library.

"Valerie, how do you feel? Do you know who this is?"

"Yes, you are Fiona. I'm so weak. Where is Bennet?"

"Right beside you, but he seems drugged. Bennet, do you know who this is?"

"Valerie?"

"No, it's Fiona. Valerie is here too. How do you feel, Bennet?"

"I'm raveling."

"Valerie, do you have any idea what happened to you in the electrical closet when you started feeling strange?"

"After the sex with Bennet. I grew very tired and I heard voices telling me to get out. But I could not. I was so tired."

"Bennet, can you telepath now?"

"Yes, Fiona. I'm coming around. We may have overdone it."

"You two get some light to re-energize. I have to go back for Jonas."

I teleported back to where I left Jonas. He had made it to the corridor and was leaning against the window at the last windowsill.

"Jonas, how are you feeling?"

"A bit better, but I can't remember ever feeling this weak before."

"Do you think that you could teleport to the lawn outside? The sun is going down, but the light would be stronger there. I'll join you in ten minutes with Valerie and Bennet."

Eventually, we were all together outside and everyone was feeling stronger. Bennet seemed to think that the stress of sex and electrical charges was sufficient to explain his and Valerie's weakness. I let it pass realizing that they were not ready to hear the real explanation for the breakdown of our AtCons—the originators were unhappy with us.

We didn't sleep that night in our usual places. Instead all four of us slept together in a back corner of the fourth floor in the Japanese and Korean stacks where no one would look for us. It was a pretty illogical move designed to make us feel safer hidden away; however, there is no hiding from the tether that links us to

the originators through our AtCons. They have made their point—
they must be obeyed.

CHAPTER 23

I woke first and noted that it was 6:30 a.m. (EST). I wondered about the weather and "heard" 30.5 degrees Celsius, partly cloudy with thunderstorms likely. That could be the weather forecast for every day in Maryland in the summer, but that I "heard" the report in Centigrade metrics was significant. Maybe things were back to normal. I woke Jonas first for a quick conference away from the others.

"You are more experienced with AtCon phenomena than I. What do you make of yesterday's loss of capacity? I'm suspicious that the same thing happened to four of us at the same time."

"I agree. I have never experienced either the weakness or the loss of standard AtCon features. I was completely helpless and, frankly, it scared me. I don't think that it was a coincidence and the only source of that kind of power would be the originators. We've been sent a warning. Now to find out if anyone else got the same warning."

"A warning about what? The only new thing done is that in the span of twenty-four hours, you and I had hot sex as did Valerie and Bennet. No one is going to give a damn about that."

"Let's check in with Valerie and Bennet to see if there have been any strange events and let them know what we learned in California."

I woke the others and we teleported to our familiar study area where we shared our theory that we had just had a warning from the originators of AtCons.

"What you say makes sense," Bennet said. "Their tether to our AtCons is like having a leash around our necks that can be jerked any time the thugs feel like it. Although scientists are reluctant to see a causal relationship where there are just correlations, correlations are where we go to inform theories. To test it, we need to check with other AtCons."

"That's what Fiona and I thought as well, but before you talk to any of the others, you should know something that we discovered while in California. While we were in a stairwell at the hospital, Fiona and I overheard Mark telepathing to Victor. The new long-distance radio wave was obviously up and running. Mark is collaborating with the Geeks Anonymous pod not only to join them, but to recruit you two and Amelia as well. The ruse to delay giving us the codes for the long-distance wave settings was to give them time to offer that as an inducement to you."

"There is no way that I would leave this pod. You are my family. " Valerie spoke with a quaver in her voice.

"What about you, Bennet? Mark is your son and the geeks have skills that can enhance your research and let you eventually communicate with your loved ones."

"And because Mark is my son, I know well his tendency to cut ethical corners when his interest is at stake. Mark's ambition trumps almost every other consideration. It worries me that he's banding with the geeks who share the same character flaw. They will reinforce each other. I don't think any good can come of communicating with the live selves directly as they intend. But even if that were not the case, I am part of Valerie's family now. You can count on me to remain with our pod."

"You realize that we will have to kick Mark out over this and neither of you could work with the geeks or him. They cannot be trusted. They are abandoning us knowing that we all face a common challenge. What will severing the partnership cost us?" Jonas was talking to Bennet now. Bennet would be aware of the Geeks' technical assets better than any of us.

Bennet spoke as though he was reading from his journal—clearly and dispassionately. "The work they're doing centers on communications among AtCons and between AtCons and live selves. Their work in communications with the living opens the door to trading their AtCon capacity for wealth and power among live selves. Mark's work in brain surgery is one example. All sorts of possibilities emerge—medical services, direct e-mail line between the living and their deceased loved ones, scientific research into advances in nanotechnology. It sounds crazy, but I believe that's what they are trying to do with the technology that they're developing."

Valerie had said little until now. "Bennet, what defense do they have against the AtCon originators?"

"They see the AtCon originators as wealthy and powerful humans far away who are not able to communicate with the living and therefore are no threat to their market share. I'm guessing they will sever their link with them and operate on the new system for communications. But teleporting requires taking AtCons through wormholes. Only Valerie seems to have a feel for that. They would probably lose their ability to teleport if they break with the originators until more research is done. That is why they would want Valerie and me. Valerie has amazing theories on the structure of the AtCon."

"What would make them think this is a good idea?" I asked.

"It isn't a good idea. They are just desperate to get back what they lost in death—their careers. The Geeks and Mark had little else in their lives. " Bennet sounded like a somber Bruce Springsteen.

Jonas added, "Like me being stuck on recovering my family. We obsess over the losses that left holes in our lives."

"Is Valerie at risk of abduction for her mind reading as well as her AtCon skills?" My words came uncensored and caught everyone by surprise.

"That will never happen. I will see to that." Jonas' AtCon was a storm-cloud grey turning darker. "Bennet, stay vigilant and close to Valerie for now. We must reconsider contacting the originators now. We have no choice that I can see."

The words were hardly sent when the prodigal son announced his presence.

"Is the whole pod here? I hope so, because I have some news that will rock your world." As if on cue, Mark's AtCon appeared out of nowhere.

"Everyone but Amelia is here," Jonas answered. "Sounds like you've got some exciting news. What's up Mark? We already know about your betrayal of the pod and your plan to join the Geeks Anonymous pod."

At that point, Amelia burst into our study with a pink AtCon the size of a beach ball.

"Good morning, everyone. Here I am for my appointment with Valerie. How were things in California, Fiona and Jonas? Oh. Are we having a meeting?"

"An impromptu meeting to hear and react to Mark's news. To catch you up, Fiona and I overheard Mark plotting with Victor to leave our pod and keep the new telecommunications capacity to themselves. I will turn the floor over to Mark now. Please feel free to rock our world, Mark."

There was a pause as I strained to catch his telepath. I sent a cloaked message to Valerie. "What is Mark thinking?"

"Valerie sending. He is totally gob smacked, but defiant. He is resolute that he will not let us see him sweat. Tell me what that means later."

"Victor has authorized me to recruit Valerie, Bennet, and Amelia to join the Geeks Anonymous pod where the long-distance communications link is available. They have other big plans for growing the pod and increasing its influence in the D.C. area. One idea that they are working on would allow dead selves to communicate with live selves. Think of it! A chance to talk to Samantha and Kate, Dad. Who wants to join me by going over now to the radio tower to talk to the three Geeks?"

Valerie spoke, "I thought you were bringing good news about Michael. How is he?"

"That contrary bitch, Michael's mother, has used her money and privilege to get him into an experimental trial for immune therapy. They canceled his surgery!"

I wasted no time weighing in. "Mark, make sure you never have to make a living in sales. Here's why. It's pretty obvious that you're no longer worth much to Victor now that his son is undergoing a therapy that you know nothing about. Sounds like your only remaining bargaining chip is to recruit Bennet, Valerie, and Amelia. And your main inducement is the mythical communication link between the living and the dead—a project that is no closer to reality than it was when it killed Valerie. But we have free will. They can decide for themselves, but just to make it official, I move that you be disbarred from this pod for sabotaging its interest in favor of your own."

"I concur," said Jonas.

Amelia spoke out next, loud and proud. "I vote you out as well even though I don't know what you did. I trust Fiona and Jonas more than I have ever trusted you. And, to save time, our marriage is over as a result of death having parted us. I am now a single mom and will no longer be known as 'Mark's wife'."

"Mark, I'll always love you, son, but you have gone too far this time. I'm opposed to the idea of interacting with the living world without research into the effects on the living and the dead. You and the Geeks are reckless in your ambitions. I'll stay here and regretfully vote you out of our pod."

"I concur. I also will remain with the pod," said Valerie.

Jonas closed off the discussion with authority. "I guess this concludes our business, Mark. Don't come around the library again. You're not welcome." Mark's AtCon disappeared.

"Well, I guess someone needs to catch me up," said Amelia, "What has Mark done now?"

"Come with me, Amelia. I will debrief you on everything while we pick out some clothes for you. Have you thought about hairstyles for your hologram yet?" Valerie led Amelia to a far corner of the archives.

NOW THAT I'M DEAD

CHAPTER 24

Jonas, Bennet, and I were left to reflect on what had happened.

"So, we have a strong five-AtCon pod but no way to communicate long distance or to the whole pod at once. As Amelia said, that may not be where our priorities should be anyhow. Tell me again, Bennet, why can't we telepath with the originators?"

"The radio wave that is our link to the 'originators' is a simple sine wave with a low frequency. These waves can travel great distances—around the world even—and are similar to what AM radio uses—'A' standing for amplitude. We just don't have the amplitude or loudness to be heard at any distance."

"Even if all our AtCons joined in together?" I asked.

"That doesn't necessarily increase the amplitude if we can't combine the sound into one wave, which means one AtCon."

"Jonas, don't you have the best auditory sensors and the biggest voice?" I asked.

Bennet interrupted, "Actually, Amelia has the strongest voice. She is a trained opera singer. Has her Bachelor's degree in voice from Vanderbilt. Before Samantha was born, Amelia split her time between auditioning and performing in various local productions and managing a temporary employment agency."

Jonas picked up on my train of thought. "This may sound crazy, but what if we combined our two strongest voices—mine and Amelia's singing voices—to send a message to the originators? If she sang into my ramped-up auditory sensors along with me, would that be loud enough?"

"Hmmm, it could. If we use both voices together at maximum volume, we might be able to send a simple message that way. Let me do some checking to see if there is anything else that would be a factor in the transmission. But it could work! You two decide on the message. It has to be just a few words, but one that will motivate a reaction." Bennet disappeared to do his research.

"Since we are dealing with a few words, I guess I'll have to do this by myself," quipped Jonas. "I have yet to hear you say much in a few words."

"Likewise, I don't recall you being much of a motivational speaker either. This may take both of us. Let's see. It must be brief and motivate them to contact us. What would that be? Hmmm. Let us talk together? Let us work together for mutual benefits? Too long. Ready to talk? Sounds like we are capitulating."

"Aren't we, Fiona? Isn't the only reason that we are trying to contact them is to turn ourselves in?"

"No, I thought we were going to negotiate to find a win-win solution to whatever is bugging them. But to do that, we need to know what their deal is, so it's a two-stage strategy: reconnaissance with an initial meeting so we know what we are dealing with, followed by a second meeting with our proposal. I did this all the time with DOD contractors.

"Check me out on my grasp of this situation, Jonas. A very powerful group has mastered the ability to capture human consciousness at the point of death and convert each one so that it remains true to that human's history as a live self. Further, the group has imposed restraints on the AtCon that houses consciousness so dead selves cannot hurt live selves or have any real effect on the natural world—a safety precaution that signifies some wisdom and foresight."

"Then you believe that they are benevolent beings who mean no harm?"

"I'm not saying that they care about us one way or the other, but they do want us to thrive and exercise free will. They allow us to communicate enough to have some companionship and let us go anywhere we want."

"Speaking of Bennet and Valerie, do you think they are a couple? As in a committed couple like we are?" Jonas sent a cloaked telepath.

I almost laughed out loud at Jonas, trying to divert my attention from a topic he does not want to discuss. "I'm glad you brought that up. No, not like us. Sometimes sex is just sex. But, they are friends with benefits and that can lead to commitment. So, are we a committed couple?"

"Are you telling me that I could have had more sex without making a commitment? Jeez."

"Are you telling me that you could have handled more sex?"

Valerie and Amelia joined us to show off their outfits. To our surprise, Valerie wore a wedding dress and Amelia wore an elaborate velvet and satin period ball gown.

"This was my costume when I sang the role of Countess Almaviva in the Marriage of Figaro," Amelia said with a swirl of her skirts.

"Fiona, why don't you wear stuff like that? Now that is pretty," Jonas bantered with a chuckle.

"Yeah, why don't I?"

"Valerie and Amelia. Bennet believes that if Amelia and Jonas sang a message as an opera together, the projection of the telepath may be great enough to reach the originators on the radio wave that connects them to our AtCons."

"I did not know that either could sing. How super cool." Valerie looked over her shoulder, obviously waiting for Bennet to notice her.

"At least in real life I could," said Amelia, beaming in her beautiful gown.

"Valerie, take Amelia to the corner and show her how to maximize her AtCon capacity. Jonas will be right along."

Jonas broke in with an enthusiastic, "I have it! 'We will help you.' Four syllables that imply that we have something to offer and that we are willing to make it available. And it provokes curiosity about what the hell we have that they might need or want." Jonas has cut the Gordian knot. Just when I think I have him figured out, he does something that is pretty amazing and useful. Maybe I'm wrong to be suspicious.

"And it also brims with good will. It is perfect." Bennet was back. "What are Valerie and Amelia doing and is that a wedding dress Valerie is wearing?"

"I will catch you up while Jonas joins the ladies to learn how to sing opera."

I turned my attention to Bennet, pleased with how things were going. At least we were finally doing something proactive. "The ladies got carried away looking through a costume ball dress catalog. They're playing an adult version of dress up. So, do you think this idea will work?"

"I refreshed my memory on radio waves and learned that there are certain conditions that facilitate radio transmissions. Most radio towers are high off the ground to get above interference from all sorts of wave busters. Also, for the same reason, transmissions from rural areas where there are fewer sources of interference help. The more isolated the location the better. A metal tower in the middle of the ocean would be perfect. That might be hard for us to manage." Bennet was excited.

"But not hard for the originators. Dubai is a modern city with the tallest buildings in the world. The whole place is built on a sand bar in the Persian Gulf. What if they are there? Could our originators be wealthy corporations aiming for world dominion?"

"What is the point of speculating? Let's send them a message and see what happens." Bennet's voice was strained. I drew comfort from our shared fears. A comfort that I have denied Jonas. Jonas is afraid of the originators! And can't admit it to me. Bennet and I are old friends so the need to assume the role of swashbuckler is moot.

"Fiona, the transmission site also has to provide us shelter while we wait for a response. We don't know how long it will take to make contact. I think a high mountain peak in an isolated area with some hotel accommodations would be best. Since we don't know how the originators may react, I would not want it to be in a place that we would hesitate to sacrifice if things don't go well. I may know a place that fits the bill.

"I once went on a skiing trip in the middle of Utah in the Tushar Mountains. Very natural and remote and some of the peaks reach three thousand meters. There are numerous little motels around and at this time of year, it should be pretty quiet. No one would find us there unless we wanted to be found."

"Tushar Mountains. Sounds mysterious. What do we do once contact is established? Here is what I was thinking. We exchange greetings and identification. Who we are by name and who they are and what they represent. Then we ask them for a copy of their rules of governance."

"What's that?"

"Well they have to be an organization of some kind—a religion, a political entity, a corporation. Whatever it is, it has a charter, or laws or articles of incorporation by which the organization and its members are governed. If we negotiate with them, we need to know their rules for operating. That would guide our strategy for negotiating and tell us something about their values. My assumption is that they are benevolent or at least have no desire to cause us serious harm. The one exception was yours and Valerie's sexual escapades that we associate with a temporary loss of AtCon powers."

"Fiona, please know that what I feel for Valerie is more than sex. I want her for my partner. But she is young and inexperienced, so I hesitate to ask."

"Bennet, can you think of anyone dead or alive who would treat her better than you will? Who would be more honest, even-tempered, kind, and generous than you?"

"No. No one. Because I am wise enough to appreciate her."

"Case closed. Let her know how you feel. Wow, they are loud. I can hear them over our telepaths. Let's go catch the show."

It took three hours, 49 minutes and seven seconds of adjusting sensors to find a way to maximize sound emission on Amelia's AtCon. With their AtCons so close as to almost overlap, Valerie's voice was feeding into Jonas' auditory sensors and then projected along with his on his AtCon radio wave. When we broke, satisfied that we had done everything possible to amplify their voices, we turned in for an anxious night, hidden in another obscure corner of the library where no one would look for us. We had two potential enemies now: the originators, pissed with our search for more power, and the Geeks, envious of our gifted Valerie.

CHAPTER 25

The next morning dawned full of promise marked by late summer's golden light. This was my favorite season in Maryland when weather is near perfect and summer flowers still bloom their heads off. The roses were giving us the season's last big hurrah right on schedule. I panned a long, slow look from the library window from my memory store before joining the pod for one last meeting to finalize preparations for our big adventure. Jonas wanted all of us to know the dangers and to be fully committed before we left.

Bennet offered to make the formal recommendation. "As everyone knows, our pod is on its own since the Geeks Anonymous pod has struck out to cut off all connections with the AtCon originators in favor of total independence and freedom to pursue their business ventures. We anticipate an adverse reaction by the originators and possibly some retaliation from the Geeks Anonymous pod. Valerie has exceptional abilities that they will need, so we particularly are concerned for her safety. I think our best course under the circumstances is to hold negotiations with the originators to see if we may coexist and even support their objectives. This assumes, of course, that their objectives are benevolent.

"The recommendation I make at this point is only to try to contact them with this message—'We can help you.' If they communicate, we will learn more and make a further decision about how to proceed. However, since we don't know who they are, only that they are powerful, we cannot assess the risk in contacting them. I would like to get a voice vote of ayes to go forward."

Everyone solemnly voted aye.

Bennet and I presented our talking points for the originators and our general strategy to the group. We agreed that Bennet should speak for our pod and we should give it a more dignified name. It took longer to agree on a name than it did the strategy and talking points. We finally reached consensus on "Touchstone" since the makeup and relationships within the pod reflected the standards of behavior that guide our lives.

With all preparations complete, we teleported to the ski lodge of the lower slopes of Mt. Baldy, a 3,685.03 meter peak. It took Jonas no time to find a section of the second floor that had been closed off for the summer. It had no electricity, but it was protection from the weather and intruders. Jonas and I took one room, which was our way of declaring ourselves a couple; Bennet took one, and Amelia and Valerie shared a third.

Valerie and I noticed a jeep advertising tours of the area parked outside. We both had the same idea.

"Hey guys," I called out to them. "Wouldn't it be smart to get some orientation to the area? Let's hitch a ride with that tour jeep. I bet it's picking up guests. We can keep an eye on possible transmission places and do some sightseeing."

We floated around the jeep until two guests and the driver appeared and settled themselves inside, leaving the back cargo hold for us. The day was beautiful—hot in the sun, but cool in the shade. The jeep took a dirt road that eventually wound up Cottonwood Canyon. To our surprise, the only forest was the scattered ponderosa pines that looked like dark green paint splotches across a brown and green canvas. True to its name, Mt. Baldy was bald. Nothing but grass and rocks adorned its rounded hump. Access to the top was a hiker's dream, paths of hard-packed dirt and gravel wending through green meadows of brightly-colored wildflowers—blue lupines, red poppies, and yellow daisy-like things. From its top, we could see for miles in every direction. Bennet exclaimed at one point, "This is like a dream. I have a really good feeling about tonight."

The paved road part of the tour took us through small towns with cheap motels advertising rooms for $36 a night, a few gas stations, and a scattering of stores. We saw very few places of entertainment—and only one or two restaurants that advertised whiskey and beer.

Back at the lodge, we met in Bennet's room. "The physical set up could not be better for our purposes. I suggest that we wait until 9:00 p.m. (MST) to make sure that everyone is off the mountain. We can teleport to the top where we were today and Amelia and Jonas can sing our message as rehearsed. We will send from 9:00 p.m. until 10:00 p.m. (MST) at 12-minute intervals. We will include the name of one of our members each time so they know who we are."

"Can they tell from our transmission where we are?" Amelia asked.

"Their command of the technology would let them trace our radio transmission; however, unless we give them our coordinates, we can't be sure that they will find us once we leave the mountaintop where we broadcast. Since the whole point of this exercise is to make contact, should we add our coordinates at the lodge at the conclusion of the transmission?"

"Let's not this first night," Jonas cautioned. "If we don't get a response by our third night, we can send them the coordinates of a house I know of on Malibu Beach, California. We can stay there and relax and figure out our next step if this doesn't work."

We were going to broadcast three nights, starting tonight—Sunday night. Everyone was edgy, excited, and distracted. Conversations started abruptly and ended in non-sequiturs. We explored the grounds of the lodge and checked out the menu. Nothing on it inspired a good food memory. Time crawled until nightfall. As the stars came out, we were stunned by the night sky, which seemed closer, a low-hanging tent of black velvet sewn with crystal spangles that shot out flashes of light in muted colors. We played around with our visual sensors at various modifications— telescopic, wide-view, zoom lenses. Each variation gave us a new picture of the skies. As we were nearly ready to leave, a meteor sent out a stream of sparkles as though there was a rent in an endlessly deep phosphorescent sea. I felt pulled by the excitement of this great adventure. I was closer to greatness than I would ever be again. Whatever happened, I would not regret my part in getting us here.

At the top of Mt. Baldy, we could see both the stars above and the sprinkle of town lights below. Occasionally, car lights on a road in a valley twinkled and disappeared. Bennet counted down from ten. Jonas and Amelia were close together. At "one," they both sang in harmony a melodic line so loud that it was painful to receive. "WE CAN HELP YOU. JONAS SMITH." Bennet repeated the countdown for the second send twelve minutes later. At the end of the hour, Jonas's and Amelia's AtCons were much dimmer and their voices were weaker. We hung around for another hour and then teleported back to our rooms.

"I guess it was unreasonable for me to think they would respond right away, but I feel let down. I'm tired and wired." Bennet moved closer to Valerie.

As if on cue, Amelia sent, "I am going to watch TV in the main lodge room. It relaxes me. Maybe someone will be eating some really good chocolate."

Jonas sent to the pod, "Fiona and I are turning in. We can gather down in the lobby in the morning and plan a fun day. If anything happens tonight, let us know. Good night, all."

In our room, we projected our holograms. I wore a fluffy terry cloth short robe with thick warm socks. Jonas had a pair of soft jeans, Docksiders, and a pale, grey sweatshirt with the sleeves pushed up. The room was dark and we could see the yellow eyes of some animal moving from brush to tree. It was stalking something. Then we heard a shrill scree as the hunted met its fate.

Jonas seemed subdued, "It's 12 degrees Celsius up here."

"I wish you hadn't told me that. Now I'm chilled. Look. I have goose bumps on my hologram legs."

"Come. Sit between my legs and I will warm you." Jonas sat against the headboard, and with knees bent, made room for me to sit. I scrunched into place and he wrapped his arms around me. I leaned against his chest. I now imagined his body heat and felt warm and secure. How marvelous the mind is.

"I hate that I can't keep you safe just like I couldn't keep my family safe from Demerson. I don't share your optimism, Fiona. I've never come out whole from an encounter with the powerful. You wondered about my abruptness when I left you at the ballpark and again at the magnolia tree. You thought it was my love for Israel that caused me to be so tentative. It was at first, but then I realized that my attachment to you has had no effect on my love for Israel. I love you both. What makes me worry about entering into a committed intimate relationship is how uncertain our existence is. Losing you as I lost Israel scares me so much that I can't be in your presence without anxiety attacks."

"You make references about memory-stealing bad dead selves and now this. What's behind your fears, Jonas? We are not powerless pawns. You are a learned man with wisdom and three lifetimes of experience. You have made a good life for yourself as an AtCon and I think I can too. We have a future together. If the originators are powerful enough to hurt us, they will. I expected nothing after death and if my AtCon dissolves in a splutter of random particles 'cause I pissed off someone, then I am no worse off than before I died. It is better to know than to be afraid. What pleasure can we take from our afterlife with some nameless fear hanging over us?"

He pulled me closer and, under his breath, said, "You are right. Night is the time when anxieties walk the earth looking for a home. Let's sleep warm and close to let our AtCons do their housekeeping. I'll feel better in the morning sun."

NOW THAT I'M DEAD

CHAPTER 26

I felt energized the next morning when I met Amelia in the lobby where the smells of bacon and coffee stimulated thoughts of breakfast. We found a table and in our hologram forms, remembered eating breakfast while we waited for the others.

"Nice outfit, Amelia. Looks like something right out of Patagonia."

"North Face. They're more stylish. This poncho is not only chic, but it has a cashmere zip-out lining and can double as a tent. I do love clothes. Your outfit is, well, authentic. You can wear anything and look good. I could never get by with baggy cargo shorts, hiking boots, and socks. Did you know that your sweatshirt has a small hole in the back?"

"It's an old favorite of mine. What are you having for breakfast?"

"That guy's western omelet with side order of hash browns and toast."

"Think I'll have the eggs over easy, bacon, more bacon, and biscuits and honey. What a treat to remember eating."

"I'm glad we can talk for a moment privately. Now that I'm dead, I'm living my dream of being a working mother with a part-time singing gig. I owe all that to you."

"Because I put you to work as pod administrator?" I asked.

"No, because you scared me into teleporting that day in Denver. You forced me to act like I had a brain and some spunk and made me try. I took a chance and when it didn't turn out 100 percent perfect, I coped. Without anyone helping me, I found solutions for simple logistics problems. I realized that I wasn't stupid as Mark had always insinuated. Now I am in the middle of this big adventure and a little scared, but also alive! Things are happening and I am part of it, not just watching life go by. However this turns out, thank you, Fiona, for seeing something in me. I only wish that Samantha knew."

"Damn, Amelia. I'm all choked up. Want some of my bacon? That poncho makes into a tent you say?"

"Look over there. It's Valerie and Bennet. I guess I would not be talking out of school to say that she never spent a minute in our room last night. I think it's cute to pretend they aren't humping like bunnies."

"Actually, Amelia, Valerie opted to room with you so you wouldn't feel like the odd person. Of course, with that good intention should go some effort to be a companion to you."

"That's so sweet, but I will let Valerie know how much I appreciate my privacy. Bennet! Valerie! Amelia sending from behind the potted plant."

They were in their AtCon rigs and fitted in neatly at our table that was nearly obscured by the overgrown corn plants. "Sleep well, guys?" I asked to let them know we were dropping the charade.

Bennet sounded stressed. "We have a bit of a problem. And there is no point in being obtuse. When we tried to hologram this morning, Valerie has my feet and I have hers."

"Fiona, I think Bennet and I may have merged in the course of copulation. We went to your room but no one is there and we have not seen Jonas anywhere. He is the only one who can help us, I fear." Valerie's AtCon was bluish grey.

"I'm sure he's around somewhere. And you're right, he does know the most about merging. You two go back to our room in case he comes back there. Amelia, you stay here and help yourself to my bacon. Keep your sensors alert and telepath as forcefully as you can for him to come to you. I will search for his AtCon around the grounds. Don't anyone teleport away from the resort."

My feeling of well-being left and in its place was another of those "what-the-fuck" thoughts about Jonas. After last night's true confessions, this has to be something else. I toured the grounds from above, looking for the telltale bluish glow common to Jonas' AtCon. I found it outside our balcony, on the ground near where we'd heard the small animal's death cry the night before. "What's up, sport?" I asked as casually as I could.

His AtCon jerked toward me. "Are you the one who told Amelia to scream for me?"

"Yeah. We have a little emergency. Can you meet me in our room? By the way, what are you doing?"

"Searching, using my high-powered visual and olfactory sensors. There's no sign of anything being killed, or even wounded here last night. Isn't that strange?"

"Well, more odd is that you're so concerned about it. Maybe the little guy got away."

"Yeah. That must be what happened. I'll head back to the room."

I collected Amelia and we joined the others in Jonas' room. Bennet and Valerie had filled him in and we were all listening to hear Jonas' solution.

"Valerie, were you reading Bennet's thoughts at the same time that you were experiencing orgasm?"

Valerie queried, "Is orgasm that part where I lose total control over my hologram and explode?"

"That's probably the case. At that moment, were you reading Bennet's mind?" Jonas asked again.

"It was longer than a moment. Last night's orgasm lasted for ten minutes and forty-three seconds. And I was reading Bennet's thoughts for the first three minutes and fifteen seconds. By reading his thoughts, I get to experience his sexy feelings along with my own. It is a real rush."

"We should have thought of this. Of course her mind-reading abilities would make a difference in how she experiences sex. It makes her even more vulnerable," I spoke quickly to keep both Jonas and Bennet focused on what was best for Valerie.

"Okay, we know what happened," Bennet said with a strained voice. "Does anyone know how to fix it? Jonas?"

"I'm guessing here, but it may be that you will have to engage in sex again and at the point of orgasm, when your AtCons are starting to overlap, you'll both have to think 'No merging.' Then maybe the merged parts will return to where they belong."

"You want me to get sexually excited to the point of orgasm with this on my mind? I may never orgasm again." Our calm, mature communicator was about to lose it.

"Oh no, Bennet. We can fix this. Sex is the bridge. We just have to manage it better. Please do not say you will not ever have sex with me again." Now Valerie has started to cry and Jonas is fidgeting.

"Can I see your holograms?" I asked.

Sure enough, Bennet's hologram had the dainty feet of a smaller person wearing vibrant violet nail polish and a thin anklet on one of the ridiculously long, thin ankles. Valerie's hologram has short thick ankles and male feet several sizes larger than her own. "You could actually get away with the difference if you wore shoes and long pants. Why don't you not worry about it today? We will stay in our AtCon rigs anyhow. Enjoy the day and have sex tonight because you want to, not to shift your feet around. Worst case scenario, Jonas will find some AtCon back home who has been through this and figure out a solution."

Amelia asked for our attention. "Well, if that crisis is resolved, I would like to teleport back to the meadow we saw as we were going up to Mt. Baldy—the one with all the flowers and view across the valley. And I want to stand there and sing 'The Hills Are Alive with the Sound of Music.' In costume."

"Cool! Anyone else have a wish? We have all day to kill, so why not enjoy it?" I said "kill." I can't believe I did that. Jonas is coming to the rescue.

"I want to teleport to the town of Beaver where there is a motel called 'Butch Cassidy.' There must be a museum or something to see there." Jonas shared his obsession with all things Butch Cassidy.

I added my wish. "I am up for both those activities as long as we can stop where we find good food. I really enjoyed breakfast memories this morning."

"I want all of you to see the lake near here. We went by it and I noted its location. I think I can guide us back there." Bennet was back. Our team was good to go.

"I am happy just to be in this beautiful, not-like-London place with the man I want to always be with. Bennet, will you marry me? Today, on Mt. Baldy while Amelia sings? "

"Yes, my true love. I will marry you, despite your ugly feet." Bennet sounded just like a raspy Bruce Springsteen.

"Okay. Assemble to catch Amelia's visualization and we will teleport to our first stop." Jonas shouted. Then as a private message to me, "Does this mean he has to look out for her now? Are we off the hook?"

The day was a dream of perfect weather and delightful companions. As Valerie in her wedding dress and Bennet in a tuxedo exchanged their vows, Amelia belted out her song loud enough that we wondered if live selves could hear. The sheer power of her voice and the music she can make with it makes me feel like fading into the foliage. No one heard the vows, but they were not meant for us anyhow.

The trip to Beaver was a hoot. It featured a cheese factory and a few bars with great nachos and beer, but the Butch Cassidy motel was a pretty conventional motel with no association with either the movie or the legend. In one bar, someone mentioned how close the Grand Canyon was, so to cheer up Jonas, we used the tourists' road map to develop coordinates for the Grand Canyon.

What we saw humbled all of us. The magnificence of this work of nature built over 17 million years ago defied our AtCons' propensity for precise measurements. All this wonder happened without man's intervention. It is ageless and permanent.

We didn't have time for more as night was falling. We teleported back to our hotel and took another look at the dinner menu. It featured prime T-bone steaks and all the trimmings. One of the guests had brought his own wine, so I also enjoyed a great glass of cabernet with my steak.

We finished in time to teleport to Mt. Baldy and watch the stars. Beginning at precisely 9:00 p.m. (MST), Jonas and Amelia sent our message to the originators, just as they had the night before. And at 10:00 p.m. (MST), Bennet anxiously waited for a response.

It didn't take long. All of us received the same telepathic message—a set of coordinates representing the longitude, latitude, and altitude of the house in Malibu.

CHAPTER 27

We gathered at the Malibu house immediately, not knowing when to expect contact or further instructions. Jonas acted as host even though, as far as I knew, he had no claim to the house. He assigned bedrooms and showed off the large deck. It was by now 9:30 p.m. (PST)—thirty minutes and twenty-three seconds since we were contacted.

As we sat on the deck listening to the surf, Bennet asked the question we all were thinking. "Jonas, do you have any idea why we were sent to this place? Does the house have some significance to either you or the originators?"

"There are times when I have come here at the direction of the originators, so I have been here several times. I brought Fiona here when we were last in California to check on Mark."

"Who are the originators, Jonas?" Bennet's voice was soft but firm.

"I don't know who they are. They appear as AtCons that look just like ours."

"How did they give you directions? And what were your assignments?" Bennet was pressing hard now for answers.

"I received a telepath just like we all did on Mt. Baldy. As far as what I did, those memories were carefully erased."

Bennet tried a different tack. "Do you know any other dead self who has had similar experiences?"

"No, I don't." Jonas answered.

I sent a cloaked telepath to Valerie. "Is he telling the truth?"

Valerie replied, "He has not lied."

Jonas teleported inside with Valerie close behind. Bennet made a move to follow, but I stopped him. "Bennet, respect her wish for privacy. Valerie has read thoughts that have upset her, so this is likely a personal matter."

"Something is not right here and Jonas may be telling the truth, but he is not telling us everything. If Valerie is upset, I should be with her." Bennet started toward the door.

"If she had wanted you with her, she would have said so. We all have to respect each other." Amelia hovered near Bennet.

"Amelia is right," I said. "Sit tight. Stay focused on our objective when they contact us again. We need to know their names, their organization, their purpose, and their rules of governance. If they want to share more information, we listen but don't comment. Nor do we answer questions other than who we are—Touchstone Pod-- and our pod pledge."

"So this is not likely to be a long meeting or accomplish much." Amelia did not conceal her distaste for the anticipated encounter.

"Amelia, by design, we want to know as much as we can before we have any substantive discussions. Then we decide what our negotiation strategy should be. Right, Fiona?"

"Right, Bennet. Let's take it slow until we know the landscape."

It was now 10:15 p.m. (PST) and the temperature drop had triggered the gas fireplace's thermostat. The light and warmth beckoned us inside where we found Jonas and Valerie in their respective bedrooms. Bennet went to check on Valerie. I left Jonas to himself as I stared into the flames of the fire and reviewed my memories—his abrupt departures when we were becoming closer

186

emotionally; steering me away from topics that may have revealed the identity of the originators; his pretense that our programmed use of precise time and distance measures and the metric system wasn't weird; our first meeting when he lied to me about who was in charge. "No one that I can tell. We are on our own." What bullshit! Now I know who he is afraid of. And why Bennet, Valerie, Jonas and I suddenly lost our AtCon abilities that day in the equipment closet. The originators were pissed with Jonas for not maintaining order in the pod. OK. So, I have a righteous beef about his withholding information, but I also have to acknowledge he had genuine cause to be paranoid. His fears of someone using his feelings for me as leverage and his oblique warning about evil doers who could take command of your memories comes from his experience with the originators. I would be as jumpy as a sore-tailed cat in a room full of rocking chairs if I had experienced loss of recent memories. It's like the folks at Potomac Gardens who have Alzheimer's.

Deep in thought, I almost missed the sound emanating from the one room in the house that was closed off. Amelia and I moved as one to teleport past the closed door. We were in a media room. There were cameras, a large projection screen, microphones, and other paraphernalia that I didn't recognize. She sent a message to Bennet to come quickly. Static emanated from speakers on the wall. "Prepare for transmission. Etaq Center for Earth Sciences grants Touchstone Pod permission to speak and be heard. Who will speak for you?"

Bennet responded. "I, Bennet Soren, will speak for Touchtone Pod. Etaq Center for Earth Sciences has permission to speak and be heard. Who shall speak for Etaq Center for Earth Sciences?"

"Jonas Smith has that distinction."

We all looked around and saw that Jonas was not with us. I teleported to our room and he was not there either. Bennet was trying to stall. "Is there an honorific that we should use in addressing your speaker?"

Minutes passed with no response. Silence had the stage. I could hear the surf outside, the metal around the fireplace expanding. Finally, a voice came back on the speaker. "There has been a change in plans. Our speaker will be His Eminence όμικρον ξι."

Bennet spoke "Your Eminence, are our thoughts reaching you clearly? We hear your voices clearly."

"Our communications system is fine, Bennet. Everyone can hear everyone. Let's continue."

"What people have designated you with such honor, Your Eminence?"

There was another long pause. "What does it matter, Bennet?"

"You first designated a dead self to be your speaker, a person we know well. Now we are speaking to a highly honored person. Are you also a dead human?"

"No. I represent an ancient people from a planet in the constellation Aquarius. It is a terrestrial planet many times larger than Earth and much older. My people, who you refer to as feces-heads, call ourselves Etaqs on Earth in tribute to the meteor showers that you have named the Eta Aquarids. We have been visitors on your planet since its oceans appeared—four billion years ago. It is unfortunate that what should have been a brief conference must now be extended to address your interminable questions, the answers to which you do not have the intellect to understand."

I had taken hologram form so I could motion to Bennet with my hands and head—stay on course.

"Then we shall only ask essential questions whose answers we are able to understand. Now that we know who you are, can you tell us your purpose for dead selves, so we can help you?"

Another three-minute pause. "The human species is destroying the Earth through overpopulation and global warming that is reducing the Earth's land mass. Contrary to the public announcements from your governments about the effects of global warming, the end is much closer than you realize—203 years, six months, twenty-four days, twelve hours, and forty-three minutes to be exact. By that time, 90 percent of the planet will be water. Life for land creatures will be over and the oceans will be too acidic to sustain most of Earth's marine life. We are trying to enhance the mental capacity of enough humans to find a solution. The 'afterlife' is a way to re-engineer humans without violating our own Alpha code that forbids interfering in the natural evolution of alien species. In this case, you are the aliens."

"I see. One more thing. Could you share with us the actual rules for governance of your activities on Earth and/or on your native planet, either in English or as a telepathic message to our memory store. We will study it and get back with you with our proposal to assist."

This time the pause was a full fifteen minutes and thirty-four seconds.

"Your request is a waste of time. We have read all your memories and tested your intellect, and although you are exceptional for humans, your intellect is a small fraction of ours. Your abilities are puny compared to ours. And your greed and lust sabotage the value of what capacity you do have. What can you possibly contribute?"

Bennet responded. "You make excellent points, Your Eminence. But you will agree that no one knows human frailties as well as humans. Perhaps there is something about us that you don't know or understand correctly? Having a copy of your rules of governance allows us to make a proposal that will be pragmatic—one that you could implement. Being informed at this point will save us time later on."

There was another pause of nine minutes and 23 seconds.

"I will grant your request even though you are not a head of state. Here are our rules sent as a telepath to Bennet's memory store. You have twenty-four hours to give us your proposal for assisting us with the global warming issue. We will convene in this room at 10:48 p.m. (PST) tomorrow. Transmission ended."

Bennet repeats, "Transmission ended."

"Let's talk in the living room. What happened to Jonas?" I was struggling to conceal my thoughts. The sonofabitch forced the aliens to reveal their identity by refusing to front for them.

"He is in your bedroom, but very small. I will show you." Valerie led the way to Jonas' room and hovered over a spot near the window. "He is on the floor where I am hovering."

I found a very small AtCon that was no more than a shadow on the floor. I sent a message, "Jonas, you kept the Etaqs from concealing their true identity. We have a chance to fix this, but we need your help. Jonas, can you hear me?"

"He is trying to answer you, but the Etaqs have programed his AtCon to view all his most frightening memories. Right now he is

189

watching his wife being lashed. He will die before he completes all the painful memories they have programmed. I must protect myself from his anguish. His pain envelops me if I get close and could harm me as well." With that she retreated to the deck.

"Bennet, we must do something. Ask Valerie what we can do!" I was frantic.

He returned quickly. "She says that you must find some way to undo the settings. Some jolt that would interfere with the Etaqs' programming."

"Let's see what happens when I merge my memory store with Jonas'. I'll try to merge AtCons to give him my strength and mix our memories. That may offset their control of his memories. If not, then I will just serve them up a ration of West Virginia temper the likes of which they have never seen before. Nothing pisses me off like a bully."

Without really knowing what I was doing, I moved as close to his AtCon as I could and opened all my AtCon sensors to seek-mode. At first I bumbled through his current visions. The metallic smell of Israel's blood came before I saw her body curled on the ground—her back a mass of torn cloth and bloody flesh, her arms over her head striped red with blood as each lash whistled through the air and ended with a crack. Motherfucking sons-of-bitches! I felt the familiar flash of anger. Always simmering near the surface, anger was my friend, my protector. Anger trumps fear and while I'm angry, fear is no longer on the table. I gave myself over to the adrenalin, reveling in the surge of power as it came—white-hot, fierce, and hungry.

The view of Israel faded and in its place I saw my father touching a sleepy child with eager hot hands and my terror when I plunged the screwdriver in his side; I saw Jennifer abandoning a sixteen-year-old girl to the streets rather than defy her bridegroom. The more painful memories I saw, the angrier I became. I fed the beast: my hatred for the people at work who made fun of my accent and K-Mart clothes, the PhDs who held my BA in contempt, and everyone who abandoned me when I filed the whistleblower complaint. And my daughters for the many times they dismissed me with rolled eyes. The will to destroy, hurt, damage; survival was primal and all-encompassing. The gate opened between my reptilian brain where my subconscious resides and the cerebral cortex where my rational thoughts and memories of my AtCon resides. I rode all my demons through that gate. Damn them! Damn them all!

NOW THAT I'M DEAD

CHAPTER 28

When I revived, it was daylight. Valerie was in hologram form and bending over me. She whispered softly, "Who are you?"

"Fiona. Fiona Campbell from Glover Gap. That is exactly who I am."

"Do you know where Jonas is? Is he in with you?" she asked.

"Fiona sending. Jonas, are you with me?"

"Hell, no. It was too crowded in there for me. I'm out here on the deck."

"So we are not merged?"

"No, but you pulled in so much compressed emotional energy that both our AtCons have altered. The good news is that I am no longer set for review of my most frightening memories. The bad news is that I may have lost all my teleporting abilities. Do you feel up to trying yours?"

I moved my AtCon around, feeling much like how Valerie described her molecular hangover. I teleported to the living room, a distance of about seven meters. I teleported to the beach below and then back up to the deck. "I'm teleporting okay. Let me get some sun and then we have to get to work on our proposal. Where is Bennet?"

Soon all of us were on the deck. "Well, how're we doing so far?" I asked.

"Valerie has some news for us," Bennet said quietly.

"I am one of them—an Etaq, an alien," Valerie spoke softly.

"I thought you might be. Your speech pattern and tendency toward literal interpretations was much like that of His Eminence. So, fill me in."

"You are not upset?" she asked.

"I just risked all to save the man who may be my worst enemy. These days, I'm working out of the right side of my brain, running on instinct. And that instinct says that you are my daughter and friend. Now's not the time to closely examine our reasons for anything. How did you get to be a little friendly alien?"

"My AtCon was embedded in a human form, probably a clone since they cannot kill a human. I must have really screwed up because they erased my memories and left me a mind-reading, sensitive child abandoned in London. The old lady I called my grandmother took me in and I lived the life that I told you about for nineteen years. When Victor met me, I was eighteen and starting to think like a computer. I was obsessed by them, probably because they resembled the Etaq AtCons in so many ways. When Victor died and tried to make contact with me, his AtCon literally triggered a reaction that stopped my heart. Dying took me back to my original form, which is why I could figure out how to do so many things earlier than other dead selves. I have a natural understanding of the AtCon that developed over maybe millions of years. I am one of them, but with very few memories of that life."

"So, our AtCons are modeled after the natural state of the Etaqs then? We were made in their image? Not very original, but logical."

"Yes," Jonas added, seemingly comfortable now with the subject. "I have seen them in their AtCons when I served as their liaison with humans. I was given a lot of perks, like the house in Malibu and enhanced sensors. In return, I served as their human image when they had to interact with people. By using electronic communications and teleconferencing techniques, I could assume infinite identities. I have seen them punish dead selves, much like they tried to punish me, but I saw nothing that would make me think they were a threat to live selves.

"I apologize for misleading you, but I saw no way that I could defy them and not lose my AtCon over it. Nor did I have any information that would have helped you. Fiona and Valerie, I love you both and hope you can forgive me."

"Jonas, you knew who was behind the AtCons and how powerful they were, but you kept information from us that would have prevented this mess. Were you my 'handler,' Jonas? Was it your job to neutralize me with romance and sweet talk? I cannot tolerate betrayal. Hear me, Jonas."

"I tried to steer you away from them, to entice you with the joys of the afterlife so you would not pose any threat to them, but you were never satisfied, Fiona. You had to know more. It was like a replay of Eve's fall from grace in the Garden of Eden. You pissed off the gods by demanding to know more."

"Look, I committed myself to you when I defied them. I am yours if you want me. But I would understand if you asked me to leave. Don't know what good a non-teleporting dead self is to you anyhow. But for whatever it's worth now, I did all I could to protect you and defend the pod. I just wasn't powerful enough."

Amelia stood in her hologram form dressed in a black jumpsuit. "I hope everyone can pick up my telepath. Jonas was there when push came to shove and he risked his life for us. I don't need any other reassurance. Besides, Jonas is a real asset against a dangerous enemy. Personal differences aside, we need all the help we can get. Let's take a vote. All in favor of keeping Jonas in our Touchstone Pod, say aye."

"I count five ayes. We have consensus." Amelia did not waste any time showing off her administrative abilities.

"Let's take a break and then we need to turn our attention to planning for tonight." Bennet exudes confidence despite learning that he is married to an alien who can't remember what she did to be disowned by her people. I marvel at this group. Even Jonas.

Bennet came over to me. "We all have read through their rules for governance while waiting for you to recover, Fiona. It's only two pages long. Our general understanding of it is this: (1) Etaqs cannot take lives of sentient beings or interfere in any way with their normal habits. Sentient beings include any living thing that can feel emotion, including fear. Since we are dead, we probably are not covered in that restriction. (2) They cannot interfere with a planet's natural evolution. We think that means they cannot directly stop the effects of human factors in global warming. They have to work through other agents, and given the restriction on what the Etaqs can do with sentient beings, dead selves are their logical agents. This also explains the restrictions that prevent us from interacting with the natural world. (3) They cannot lie. Period. To anyone, and we think that includes dead selves. (4) Punishment to their own is administered through a series of hearings with tribunals that is so tortuous that we assume it must be a rare event. We concluded that they are largely a homogenous society predisposed to order and civility."

"May I speak?" Jonas asked. "What I can add is that their behavior is always rational. I have never seen them demonstrate any real emotion. It's almost like they don't have feelings. They certainly are not given to violence and actually are repulsed by sexual contact between humans. They view it as vulgar and disgusting."

"Jonas, what do you know about their numbers here on Earth? How many are we dealing with?" Amelia asked.

"I have only met five different alien AtCons since I began serving as their spokesperson. On those occasions, I transmit by voice what they send me by telepath, only I use the appropriate accents and slang. Besides English, I speak fluent French, Spanish, Italian, and German."

"Then there must be other dead selves to represent them to Chinese, Russians, and other nationalities. Still, it is a smallish operation." Amelia seemed thoughtful, as if learning about the smaller numbers had lessened her fear.

"Do we know anything about their lives on their own planet? If they're disgusted by sex, how do they procreate?" I ask out of curiosity.

Valerie, quiet up to this point, let us know that she had been processing all that has happened too. "They cannot die, so they don't need to procreate. Their AtCons can no doubt do all the things that Bennet theorized—move objects, communicate any distance and to any number of receivers. They may even be able to teleport through outer space. Think of our skills and multiply them forty times over and then throw in mind reading, since I am sure that is an innate feature or they would have abolished it with my memories. I suspect that there are human clones embedded with Etaq AtCons working as their agents in large numbers. The only problem with that is we still communicate very literally. We are misfits among humans. Jonas may have been an experiment to see if a dead self AtCon hologram could more realistically imitate a human." Valerie looked up at Bennet as she spoke, perhaps to see what affect her alien status was having.

"They are all intellect, brilliant beyond our comprehension, yet our AtCons are only slightly more intelligent than when we were alive. The AtCons don't seem to affect intelligence or does it? Jonas, you are the longest dead. Have you become smarter over time?" Bennet and Valerie were in hologram form now and sitting close with arms around each other.

"Good question. Yes, in a way. The more I studied and learned, the easier it was. The first baccalaureate degree took me three years, going at it full time. That would be normal for adult humans. Toward the end, I took three degree programs simultaneously. My ability to absorb and retrieve information is much better now. I also noticed that I can use my sensors to take readings of living tissue and that I know what the readings signify based on a Freshman survey course in biology. For example, I can scan an injured frog and know what internal parts are injured and whether poison, disease, or trauma was the cause. When I was up your nose before you died, Bennet, I knew that the oxygen levels in your blood were too low and your blood carried too much waste.

"What may be more interesting is what has not changed in me. When I was alive, I could play a harmonica. I still can, but not much better than I ever could. When Amelia taught me to project my voice in preparation for our amplification exercise, I sang some spirituals and sounded exactly as I remembered, but no better. When I chose the classes at the University of Maryland, I had no interest in the arts and even the architecture course I took bored me. That despite my pleasure at making furniture and working with wood when alive."

"The AtCon is less receptive to the creative arts. But Valerie is very attuned to visual arts. Valerie, care to comment?" I asked.

"I am very drawn to the paintings in the library, pictures in the periodicals. Sometimes, I view them over and over in my memory store. I was afraid for anyone in the pod to know, although no one has ever expressed any interest in what I look at, so I do not know where that came from unless it is some vestigial memory as an Etaq."

"Guys, I'm starting to fade," I spoke with a hoarse voice that Linda Ronstadt would not recognize. "I need some rest. We all do. Our opponents have set an arduous task for a time when we're normally in deep sleep. Let's get some sun on the deck while we think about what we know about the Etaqs and their purpose. Each of us has a different filter for the same information, different ways of looking at things. Then let's meet at 6:00 p.m. (PST) to plan our strategy for tonight."

"Will Bennet handle the presentation tonight as he did last night?" asked Amelia.

I answered. "No. We will all participate tonight."

CHAPTER 29

I felt confident that I had found the Achilles' heel of the Etaqs, but was cautious about sharing that. We were on their turf surrounded by sound equipment, a former Etaq who can read minds, and a dead self who worked for them. Although Jonas and Valerie's candor in answering my questions reassured me, I was taking no chances. Surprise is something I was certain the Etaqs were unaccustomed to and we needed every advantage. My strategy will require contributions from all five of us. By having them concentrate on the relevant information, their data retrieval systems will be attuned for the contest tonight. There was no doubt in my mind that the Etaqs were coming to put us in our places. They may not be emotional, but they understood the leverage of fear. Of all the dead selves that the Etaqs could have recruited to serve as their human interface, they picked a former slave who had been brutally abused.

At 6:00 p.m. (PST), we met on the deck to watch the sun drop and feel the cool breeze off the water. "Pod, keep in mind that this is the home of the Etaqs. Use only language that they would not find offensive here. Guard your tongue as though the neighborhood gossip has his ear to the door. Got me?

"First, we need to realize that they take literally what we say, much like Valerie does. During the meeting, choose your words carefully when you need to speak to the group. Jonas will listen for such instances where there may be confusion and interject to interpret or restate the remark. He is most sensitive to their language issues. I will facilitate the presentation to keep us on track to make our points. Bennet will monitor me and redirect my remarks if I get off course. On my cue, Amelia will sing. Amelia, what is the most rhythmic, passionate song in your repertoire?"

"'Habanera' from Carmen."

"Be ready to sing that tonight."

"In costume?" she asked.

"Hmmm. May overwhelm them. Jonas, how would the Etaqs react to a passionate, exciting song sung by Amelia who was also showing bare legs and lots of cleavage?"

"May put them in some sort of swoon. Just sing."

"You're right," I said.

"Now that I have your curiosity up, my proposal is quite simple. The Etaqs are geniuses at gathering, analyzing, and retrieving information. But they have two flaws. The obvious one is their reliance on telepathic communication or reading each other's minds, which leaves them oblivious to the nuances of idiomatic language and the role context plays in the meaning and interpretation of language. So, some of their data must be misunderstood coming in and misstated going out.

"The second flaw is that as their intellects have grown, whatever innate second sense or intuition has atrophied. They now are totally dependent on a super brain or what Bennet referred to as a 'computorium.' A lot of animal instinct was lost to us as well,, but we still have some left. It allows our brains to have epiphanies and be creative. They lack that. And without it, their analysis of the information follows conventional, highly-structured processes, like a computer would. Although we have computers that can win at chess and even Jeopardy, we don't have one that can write a poem or compose a hit song. Our ability to add creativity to their analyses and improve their interface with humans is what we have to offer."

"One last point. According to their remarks last night, the Etaqs have been here for as long as we've had a climate; however, they have not been able to achieve their goal of preventing humans from destroying the planet. They are failing, which makes them amenable to a new idea."

"Brilliant!" Bennet fairly shouted. "Once you spelled it out, I could see it as well. Physicists who have made the greatest contributions to science were the ones who had a revelation, like Stephen Hawking. You are right, Fiona, if the Etaqs were so smart, what explains their failure to affect change after working at it so long? They are missing something. And I bet our team could figure it out. Damn. I was worried but now I'm excited."

Jonas spoke up. "When you asked me about what changed in my intellect, I got so busy answering the question that I failed to share this. As my store of knowledge grew, I could solve more kinds of problems, but not solve any one any faster than I could as a slave. Information can grow but the ability to apply it to solve problems requires something that we can't get from our AtCons."

"And I am going to demonstrate creativity by singing a song that they can't have a match for," added Amelia.

"That's the idea, but I don't know what their music is like. Hard to imagine that their civilization is devoid of art and music completely. But if 'Habanera' doesn't do it, you should have something else in your repertoire." I listened as they continued to share their ideas.

Valerie joined in. "I don't seem to have a particular role to play in the presentation."

"Yes, you do. I'm going to try to get them to sit with us around the small conference table in the media room in hologram form so we can observe their body language. Even if I'm successful, I want you to sit near me so you can share what you are picking up from them. You are our only mind reader."

"The fireplace is on and it is cool out here. Let's go inside and relax by the fire and await their contact. Say nothing about this inside the house. Just in case they have a way of listening to us."

NOW THAT I'M DEAD

CHAPTER 30

The hours passed quickly thanks to Jonas telling jokes and Jonas and Amelia singing blues songs. Everyone had adopted holograms with wardrobes that represented their unique personalities. Bennet wore a poet's shirt with bloused sleeves and skinny black pants with black leather shoes. He looked like something out of a production of Romeo and Juliet or a Renaissance Faire. Amelia wore an emerald-green velvet gown with short sleeves. To hide her manly feet, Valerie had chosen a pair of wide-legged jersey lounging pajamas in dark purple with red sequined accents. She had a purple Mohawk haircut and a nose ring. Jonas wore his jeans, red boots, sleeveless vest, and Stetson hat. I wore jeans, a bulky knit cotton sweater, and my hair in a smooth pageboy cut. We were ready. The time was 10:48 p.m. (PST). This time no static alerted us to their presence.

"His Eminence, όμικρον ξι, is ready to commence the meeting between the Etaqs and the Touchtone Pod."

"Bennet here. As you can see, we are assembled around your conference table in our hologram forms. Would you please join us?"

"Is that necessary?"

"Bennet here. Humans communicate through body movements as well as with spoken language. Etaqs use both telepathy and mind reading. It seems that we function at a disadvantage otherwise; unless, of course, you can disengage your mind-reading apparatus."

"Do you think we can read minds from such a distance?"

"I cannot answer that question since I know neither the distance that you reference nor the nature of your capacity for mind reading. We have disclosed our ability to read body movements and we assume you can read minds since Valerie can."

"My counsel of advisors will convene at the conference table then. In hologram form."

Immediately, we saw nine forms clothed in long, grey robes with hoods that concealed their faces. They looked like monks from the middle ages. One wore a robe with a black drape over the shoulder. He took the elevated seat at the head of the table and was flanked by four others on either side. We moved to make room for them and arranged ourselves so that Bennet sat opposite His Eminence. I sat to Bennet's left, with Valerie to my left. Jonas sat to Bennet's right, with Amelia to his right. There was an empty seat between the two factions on both sides of the table.

What happened next caught our pod by surprise. His Eminence rose to speak.

"The Etaqs do not enter these discussions with goodwill. With the exception of the one you call Valerie, you are all here as a result of our magnanimous gift of AtCons to house your consciousness when you died. Yet you insult us by calling us feces-heads and you have the audacity to imply that we need your help and you are entitled to see our charter of ethical behavior— our 'rules of governance.'" These rules oblige us to hear your petition and to judge your case fairly; however, should you fail to make a case for your value to our mission, or raise doubt as to your worthiness to be endowed with an AtCon, the following punishments will be meted out.

"Bennet and Amelia. Our review of your memory stores shows that you two are the least offensive of the group. Except for Bennet's sexual obsession with Valerie, he shows potential to join our group of dead selves who are research acolytes. There he will work on challenges of great importance to Earth and thousands of universes alongside the deceased great earth scientists of the past two thousand years.

"Amelia, your dedication as a mother and your modesty as a female would make you a welcome worker in our juvenile AtCon school. This is where juvenile dead selves are cared for until they can fend for themselves.

"Jonas. Your betrayal of our earlier agreement is unprecedented. That Fiona effectively stopped your punishment is but a temporary reprieve. You will resume viewing your painful memories as a slave until you choose to give up your AtCon and pass on to the great void.

"Fiona. Of all the dead selves, your memory store has the greatest collection of outrageous character flaws and personal failures. You killed your own father and fled your home and family to seduce a man and conceive two children that you could not care for properly and who now have no respect for you. You were almost fired from your job and ended your career as a despised and incompetent member of your work group. Your life is devoid of accomplishments or value to society at large or your circle of acquaintances. You are neither loved nor lovable. Your punishment is to be bound to your dead father until he forgives you and then pass on to the great void.

"Valerie. We have no choice but to allow you to resume your existence as one of us since that is, in effect, what you are. But if participation in this farce is any indication of your unrepentant nature, then you will be taken back to our home planet for trial with my recommendation that all your memories be erased and all your sensors not essential for life be detached."

Before anyone could react, Valerie loudly exclaimed, "Fuck you! I denounce my Etaq origins. I am now a human female dead self. My mother and father are human dead selves. My husband is a dead self. This pod is my family. And you better be careful, because our sum is greater than our parts. We are not afraid of you so just cool it, hotshot."

His Eminence and his advisors froze, literally. They stopped all movement.

"Valerie, what are they thinking?" I asked while looking straight ahead.

"There are only five AtCons present. The others are just holograms with no thoughts at all. Something is screwy. I think His Eminence is in shock and is on a direct circuit with the other four AtCons. For all practical purposes, you are dealing with just one mind spread among five AtCons. I am picking up anger, but also uncertainty. I spoke up because I knew the rest of you felt as I did and I wanted to distract them from reading your minds. And it is better that they direct their anger at me. I am less essential to our mission. I made a strategic decision, did I not?"

"Yes. And a noble one at that. I will take it from here."

"Your Eminence has made many good points in their opening remarks," I spoke in a soft voice hoping that it would convey calmness. "When gender of a human is uncertain, we use the plural pronoun out of respect.

"Let me begin my opening remarks with a correction. No one here used the term 'feces head.' That is not a term in common use among humans speaking the English language. The correct term is 'shithead'. It is a term of endearment that typically refers to a reckless youth. If you check your memory stores, it is a term we used to refer to our colleague and friend, Mark Soren, when we discovered his involvement with the Geeks Anonymous Pod's communication system. Your interpretation of 'shit' as feces is understandable, but is an example of the complexity of the English language for people who are non-native speakers. 'Shithead' is an idiom and English is a very idiomatic language.

"Nearly all countries and cultures of Earth speak some English. It is the language used for all cross-cultural transactions and the most common language among the educated, which includes the people who will determine the leadership of your effort to stop global warming—scientists, mathematicians, engineers, and technology users of all kinds. According to several authoritative sources that I consulted, 80 percent of all electronic communications on Earth are in English. Four of our pod are masters of the English language, having published technical documents in that language. Valerie is learning quickly and had her memory not been erased, could probably qualify as a highly-educated person as well.

"One of the ways we can help you is to serve as translators to assure the complete accuracy of your data and any written reports that you may need to compile and share with humans.

"At risk of stating the obvious, we are also citizens of the most powerful country on the planet. With the exception of Valerie, we are Americans who certainly know how our countrymen think and the dynamics that motivate our society's cultural shifts. For example, I would guess that you have been sending scientific articles to support an immediate response to the threat of global warming to heads of state, such as our President. We would have advised you to direct your attention instead to large multi-national businesses. First, you need a global response, not national. Second, all business depends on capital investments largely influenced by the major financial institutions that are also global.

"If your main argument is that in a little more than two hundred years, Earth will be 90 percent water, you are doomed to failure. Here is why. Your timeline is too distant. As an ancient people who have a history counted in millions of years and whose span of time as individual conscious entities is indefinite, your sense of time is much different than what humans would have. We have only existed as a species for two hundred thousand years and our lives are over in less than ninety years. For us, the only time of any consequence is the span between the present moment and the probable death of our youngest progeny.

"For global business, the time span of consequence is from the present until the next stockholder's meeting—less than a year. If you want quick action that is comprehensive and global, you must appeal to global businesses by showing them how they can make money by ameliorating actions that contribute to global warming. For example, I'm sure your databanks are replete with facts that could be integrated to make a strong case that insurance companies stop insuring waterfront properties right now. And how clean energy sources can be more efficiently exploited by a carbon-based fuel industry to stimulate higher profits than they receive from fossil fuels. With this change in strategy and our help bridging the language barrier, you could reduce carbon emissions drastically in one year and launch the technology that can effect corrections of the damage already done."

"If your critique of our strategy is correct, why should I need your help beyond this?" demanded His Eminence.

"An excellent question, Your Eminence. According to your statements, you have been working on the issue of helping humans evolve faster to prevent catastrophic damage to the planet for about two thousand years. That would be since the approximate death of Jesus, the Nazarene. Am I correct?"

"Yes. When our experiment of introducing a more humane religion—Christianity—failed to mitigate human excesses, we started working on dead selves one at a time. As a research experiment, the corruption of Christianity provided valuable insights into civilization at that time, just as our experiment with dead selves is yielding valuable data today."

"Your ideas had merit and your implementation was flawless until the human power brokers got involved and restated Christian principles. We concede that the Etaqs are great thinkers whose ability to retain and retrieve information is many times greater than ours. "

"Forty-five times greater." His Eminence's chief advisor clarified.

"Exactly! And for that reason, you do not use and may have lost your long ago instinctive memories and capabilities. For example, the monarch butterflies migrate from the United States to Mexico every year without the benefit of much of a brain. Right?" I was on a roll.

"The correct name is Danaus plexippus. And it is the United States of America, to be exact."

"Thank you, chief advisor. This little butterfly, migratory birds, and many mammals still depend on innate, instinctive memories for survival because they have small brains. As a species' brain takes over more of its survival tasks, its instincts and innate memories atrophy, as an unused appendage will over time. The Etaqs are so evolved that they depend exclusively on their superior brains. Humans, because we are less evolved, still have vestiges of our instincts remaining. We call it intuition or creativity.

"Problem solving depends on analysis of data. Right?"

"Right." The chief advisor allowed.

"Human analysis mixes intuition and creativity to make analytic leaps to correct conclusions. This lets us to not only solve problems, but also to create art, invent new things, and discover solutions that may not show up from the analysis of data alone.

"Let me show you an example of human creativity. I present Amelia singing a song written by another human 139 years ago."

Right on cue, Amelia stood, moved away from the table about three meters, turned sideways, smiled coquettishly, and sang the first notes of 'Habanera.' The notes were crisp, setting the rhythm. As the pace quickened, Valerie's mezzo soprano voice played with frequencies that showcased her control of timbre. Her voice held us captive as one note after another resonated through our sensors. Then her body began moving with the music. Amelia might not have been in costume, but she acted out the role of a seductress.

I watched the Etaqs. Their faces behind the hoods were directed toward Amelia. Their robes rustled and seemed to float out from their bodies. The song lasted five minutes and eighteen seconds as Valerie's voice overpowered the room. The quiet that followed lasted longer.

Finally, I broke the silence. "Saving the planet from us humans is a lot of work. Wouldn't you like some help? You have made a brilliant step in that direction with the research acolytes, but science is just one piece of the solution. There is room for dead selves with leadership skills and business acumen, scientists who understand economics and social institutions, and artists who are creative. It's a job that requires diverse talents and imagination."

His Eminence spoke. "It is true that we have all the facts that you referenced, but somehow we arrive at wrong conclusions. How is that possible?"

Bennet spoke. "Your Eminence. Your context was not the right context for the problem you were solving; your analysis is correct, but had no relevance. Therefore, your solutions didn't work. We cannot make such a mistake, because we are the context."

Jonas spoke. "When you described Fiona as a failure, you did not look at the context. Success is not determined by chance events over which there are no control; success is making the most of what chance provides you. Fiona grew up with no mother and an abusive father, persevered, and learned enough to survive without friend or family. Then she went on to acquire an education and raise her children to be effective adults. Fiona changed the future of all her progeny. She broke the cycle. In that context, she is a highly evolved and successful human."

"What is your decision, Your Eminence?" Bennet asked.

"My decision rests on the answer to this one question. Fiona, is it really true that 'shithead' is an endearment?"

"Your Eminence, it wasn't when we first said it, but it is now." I spoke with all the glory of Linda Ronstadt's mellifluous voice.

"As your chief advisor, Your Eminence, I have completed a data check and all said is accurate. I might also note that the music would be highly valued on our home planet if you think it is not too . . . too . . . passionate."

Amelia raised her hand to get the notice of His Eminence. "Your Eminence, is there no music on your planet?"

"Oh, yes. Of course. Music stimulates our intellect to such an extent that we have to limit it to less stirring strains of earth music. We started exposing Etaqs to Gregorian chants when the first recordings were available. Since then we have worked our way up to Bob Dylan. His lyrics enthrall our citizenry. My assistant's question is whether Miss Amelia's music is too great a leap.

"We have many things to consider, but on the whole, your proposal has value. My advisors and I must construct a plan for implementing your ideas when you are rested. This has been an exhausting event on both sides that we will be analyzing for some time. Much was learned this night. We will leave you to the hospitality of the house and will contact you soon. Adieu."

* * *

It was hours past midnight. My eyes burned. I absentmindedly massaged the sharp pain along the back of my neck that meant I had been sitting at the keyboard too long. I walked out to the deck overlooking the Pacific. The salt air and fresh breeze felt good. The sound of the surf was soothing.

"Do you trust them?" Bennet had asked that night. "No," I had replied. "Trust comes with time." I had forgotten all about time, the fourth dimension; but the Etaqs had not. What did Jonas say? "For them, time is a toy."

My next conscious moment after that was finding myself in the house alone, in human form as a live self, but two years earlier—2012. I spent the night writing down all my memories about the meeting before they faded. I no longer had a memory store. The Etaqs had sent me back in time.

With no idea what to do next, my live self exhausted and craving sleep, I opened the windows in one of the bedrooms and crawled into the bed. The sheets were at least 800 thread count and silky to the touch. Mixed with the sound of the surf was a humming noise, a tuneless kind of meandering singsong that eased my anxiety as sleep pulled me down into blissful mindlessness that I had no will to resist.

NOW THAT I'M DEAD

CHAPTER 31

The next morning, the doorbell woke me. By the time I recovered from the surprise and found something to put on, there was no one there, but a box attested to a delivery. Inside was a selection of every version of Starbucks coffee made and a French press. I wasted no time indulging myself in my one addiction while exploring the small but well-equipped kitchen. The freezer section held a very chilled bottle of expensive gin; my choice of martini fixings were in the fridge along with boxes of expensive dark chocolate—all tips to my food preferences easily found in my AtCon memory store. On the counter by the phone was a stack of menus from restaurants that deliver and a credit card in the name of C. de Agnés. I was getting the VIP treatment from the Etaqs. My hunch was right. They have a plan for me.

I had a chocolate truffle with another cup of coffee and logged onto the laptop I found in the media room. Carlotta de Agnés had numerous e-mails as an undisclosed recipient. They all referred to an upcoming International Symposium on Global Warming's

Implications for National Security to take place at the Fairmont
Hotel in San Francisco on September 13-14. Heads of state from
fifteen countries that represented the world's best-funded military
powers were meeting to hear new findings from the latest research
on global warming. The subject of this latest round of e-mails was
whether military contractors would be permitted in the audience. I
did not respond on behalf of Carlotta. After all, "Carlotta" could be
someone else who uses this house or even a cover for Jonas. I did
read through the attached files that included a tentative agenda and
some of the papers that were being presented.

The chocolate truffle wore out halfway through a paper on
"How Estimates of Carbon in Soil Can Affect Global Warming
Computer Models." I took a break, arranged for a pizza delivery
and had a hot shower in a luxurious bathroom where the view from
the toilet was a panoramic expanse of ocean. In the adjoining
bedroom's closet were clothes that fit perfectly. Most were
imported from Italy and some had labels that even I recognized.
There was also a pair of khaki cargo pants of softest cotton and a
selection of T-shirts and sandals. My host apparently anticipated I
would need a large and expansive couture wardrobe, but also knew
my preferences for casual wear. It would be too much of a
coincidence that the mysterious Carlotta and I were the exact same
size now that I'm a matronly seventy-four once again. Apparently,
I'm appearing at the symposium.

By mid-afternoon, I was reading without paying attention, so
stopped and sat on the deck to process what I had learned about
this symposium so far. First, it was international but limited to the
countries with the greatest percentage of GDP invested in military
expenditures. This group included the United States, United
Kingdom, France, Germany, Brazil, Japan, India, China, Russia,
South Korea, Australia, Italy, Saudi Arabia, the United Arab
Emirates, and Turkey.

Second, the agenda made it clear that the presentations were
focused on how global warming would affect these countries'
defenses and ability to wage war. At least one presentation posed
questions about how rises in sea level would affect seaport
infrastructure and the ability of a country to maintain naval vessels
where they are currently based. Another presentation optimistically

touted global warming a way to end war. And that was when I had an idea.

I Googled "Etaq" and found not only a website, but also an e-mail address for the Etaq Center for Earth Sciences (ECES). Carlotta sent the ECES an email referencing the paper on how carbon release in soil will affect computer model for global warming. It included a simple message: "How solid is this research?" The almost instant response was—"It's ours." That meant it will stand up to any scrutiny. I re-read the paper and then researched effects of rising sea levels on the Norfolk, Virginia Naval Station. Home for the Atlantic fleet and the largest naval shipyard in the world, it has already experienced the effects of climate change because of its unique location relevant to Gulf currents and area topography. If only there was a way to make this example relevant to the other countries using the new computer model that incorporates carbon release factors. My words to the Etaqs came back to haunt me. "You have to make it a current problem that has immediate financial implications." How clever that they have turned the challenge back to me. So, how do I do that?

My brain answered, "not tonight." Experience had taught me the treachery of fatigue, which is like working drunk. But there is no harm in relaxing with a martini as long as I don't touch the computer or use dangerous equipment. The thought of a cold martini with melba toast, cream cheese, and caviar lightened my mood. As I added another great memory to my collection, a sense of optimism flooded over me. Yes, maybe the great gin, but nevertheless it was a good way to end another day as Carlotta de Agnés.

NOW THAT I'M DEAD

CHAPTER 32

The following morning, I took my coffee to the terrace and breathed deeply of the salt air as the sun burned off the last of the mist. The beauty of this planet must be unique for the Etaqs to invest so much in its protection. After the second cup of Starbucks and 20 minutes of being mesmerized by the pitch and roll of ocean swells, I shouted out loud, "Stupid! "The key is to employ the Etaqs' time travel capes to show humans before and after pictures of what has happened in the last 50 years and then, based on the new computer modeling, what further damage is coming. Then convert that to costs related to each nation's GNP. The Etaqs can copy actual photos and cite records for naval installations of each country. That would be both dramatic and current.

My fingers flew over the key board as I typed out the request. "Etaq Task 1--Provide pictures of two of each country's largest naval facilities as they appeared 50 years ago; United States, United Kingdom, France, Germany, Brazil, Japan, India, China, Russia, South Korea, Australia, Italy, Saudi Arabia, the United

Arab Emirates, and Turkey. Pictures and actual sea levels must be authenticated by record source.

Etaq Task 2—Provide current—2012--photographs and sea levels for same sample with same documentation standards.

Etaq Task 3—For the same sample and using the revised computer modeling adjusted for effects of carbon release from soil, project the sample of naval facilities sea levels in five years—2017--and 20 years--2032. Provide artist rendering of effects if no photos exist. Show costs for installation repair or replacement as a proportion of GNP. Use citations for peer review.

A response came back within an hour "Would you prefer a range with probabilities for each?"

I replied, "Disregard probabilities. Too much print on a slide and we have a font too small to be read by the larger audience. Let's keep the main thing the main thing. That should be a graph for all countries in the sample and, for each, the sea level change for their respective installations over the course of the next five years and then the next 20 years. Now, this is the important element of the presentation. Using visual reference points that can be seen today, give me pictures of what this will look like. What I'm trying to achieve is a before and after comparison of the effects of global warming statistically for the scientists and in pictures for the non-scientists."

The results came back that afternoon. Based on the projections of carbon release, rises in sea level would result in a third of the countries losing their naval installations by 2017. By 2032, rising sea levels would render all the naval installations useless across all the countries. The results were better than I had imagined. I sent one last e-mail before calling it a day. "How would this one factor influence each country's ability to ship and receive goods and subsequently their GDP?"

That should keep them busy for the next twelve hours while I enjoy a cold martini and Kobe steak dinner. Hope the take-out place can rustle up a good Malbec with that.

CHAPTER 33

The next two days were spent pouring over the reports from ECES and the information on the symposium. There were three types of participants invited—heads of state or their designees from each of the selected countries; researchers like Carlotta, who would be presenting results of their research: and, as of today, businesses acting as military contractors. The symposium sponsors allowed each country to bring their top five contractors in terms of contract revenues for the past fiscal year as long as no one corporation was represented by more than one person. Interesting. Out of fifteen countries polled, there were only twenty corporate representatives registered at this point. It was unclear which country was associated with each one. Included as business registrants were the usual major technical and heavy manufacturing concerns, arms manufacturers, and information technology giants. Most were American.

But when I checked the Fairmont Hotel website, there was no mention of the symposium. I checked the dates again. Either the e-mails are bogus and I'm being set up, this is a dry run, or this meeting has gone black by design.

On a hunch, I called the Fairmont to check the reservations of Carlotta de Agnés on those dates. The very polite and efficient clerk confirmed the reservation. The safest option is to assume it is happening and I will play a major role in ECES's presentation impersonating Carlotta de Agnés. The agenda did not list details of presentation schedules, which may allow me to engineer a late time for our presentation and thus piggyback on other presentations to build momentum. The later in the program, the better. I e-mailed that recommendation to ECES and returned to my preparations.

Another three days passed. A detailed final schedule for meeting events showed ECES making the final research presentation on the second day. The Etaqs must be able to manipulate any computer system to do its bidding. I sent the Etaqs a draft of my PowerPoint slides with directions for data in graphic form, photographic illustrations needed, and their placement. I was nervous about the slides. This presentation had to connect with its audience on both intellectual and emotional levels, which required more than data analysis skills on ECES's part.

With the presentation four days off and nothing to do, I took the night off and finished the Argentinian Malbec on the deck, wrapped in a throw from the sofa and watching the stars while fog rolled in. The display of the sheer power of ocean waves pounding the beach as fog forms hills of tumbling grey mist is eerie. Soon there would be no visibility from where I sat. The fog would obliterate it all, even the glittering night sky would disappear along with evidence of my existence.

I thought again about calling my daughters. The first time I lived these days was in my own home still. Would they notice the strange number on their caller ID? What excuse could I give for not being at home—spur of the moment invitation from an old friend in LA? Could I pull that off? Probably, but what would be the point unless I had something to say to them. I'm sorry that I disappointed you, but I really loved you more than life itself. Doesn't that count? My choices seemed either banal or dramatic or just plain stupid because they are too late. The occasion for a conversation about my feelings for them passed long ago. Timing is everything. Opportunities to capitalize on a perfect segue disappear in one tick-tock. What would be different if I had taken them in my arms after the bike ride and thanked them for the best time of my life? Told them they were my favorite people? Told them the truth about my demotion? How did I come to this—feeling so hat-in-hand around my children? Like I wasn't good enough for them.

My daughters have no idea what they owe me for running away from my father and Glover Gap. But, then, why would they? Thanks to me, there is nothing in their world that would give them even a clue that people lived as I did. And, if I am successful with this presentation, they will never know my part in giving their great-grandchildren a chance to live. But I will. And that will have to be enough. Besides, the Etaqs took a risk sending my AtCon back in time to do this. Exposing them or making an imprint on the future that they cannot control is too great a risk. The less I vary from their plan, the better. The mission has to remain my priority.

Chilled by the damp, but warmed by the wine, I stared off toward the ocean, wondering what was hiding in the fog.

* * *

Two days later, ECES e-mailed a video file. It was my presentation, complete with background music! It was a genius morphing of visual and auditory media into a dramatic representation of statistical data. There had to be humans translating my slides to the Etaq video technicians. Only Amelia could have done that, which meant that my team was on the other end of the ECES e-mails.

I sent my compliments and made notes in a few places for changes. I also asked for an addendum listing all the scientists who were on record for concluding that human factors were affecting climate change and all scientists who took the opposite position.

Nothing to do now but wait. I watched television, sunbathed, ate well, napped often, and generally readied myself for any possibility.

The morning before the meeting commenced with the startling sound of a ringing phone. It was a limousine service confirming a pick-up for 3:00 that afternoon. I had expected that the Etaqs would have arranged the logistics and I was ready. I wore one of the Chanel suits and my briefcase contained the laptop with the presentation queued and copies on two different thumb drives.

The limo drove an hour to a private airfield where the chauffeur assisted me to the stairs of a small jet. A young woman seated me in a plush leather chair while my bags were stowed and the engine revved into a high-pitched roar. Once in the air, she brought me a sealed envelope and asked if I would like refreshments. As she fetched me some Champagne, I opened the envelope. Inside were $500 in small bills, a passport with my picture and Carlotta's name, confirmation of my hotel reservation, a credit card identical to the one in the house, and a letter authorizing Carlotta to represent ECES at the symposium. At this point, I was beyond surprised. I was in the hands of geniuses with incredible resources. All I had to do was make the presentation the day after tomorrow.

CHAPTER 34

The first day of the symposium was uneventful. I observed the presenters, made notes where their data supported mine, and watched the reactions of the national representatives to the presentations. Since the meeting room was cyber secure, no one had Internet access or cell phone service. Representatives around the conference table easily revealed when something peaked their interest by making notes. Likewise, doodling and staring vacantly into space signified boredom. Using this system, I readily determined that the presentation about how global warming heralded a new era for peacemaking was definitely a ho-hummer.

That evening, I skipped the cocktails and dinner social given by the defense contractors. Although drinks and dinner are impotent bribes, the arrogance of the contractors grated my every nerve; nor could I take even the slightest risk that anyone would recognize me from my Defense Department days. I wanted the advantage of surprise tomorrow.

There was a subtle shift in the tone of the meeting on the second day. Whether it was the social event that previous night or some other political nuance known only to insiders, cliques were forming. Country representatives were passing notes back and forth. Brazil, Saudi Arabia, the United Arab Emirates, and Turkey were in communication during the morning session and sat together at lunch. The United States, United Kingdom, France, Germany, and Italy huddled during the morning break and then during lunch. Australia, normally part of the US-European group, aligned instead with Japan, South Korea, and India. China and Russia were either isolated or aligned as a somber duo. They interacted with no one. The audience of contractors was called to order from their noisy sidebars several times and earned a scorching rebuke from the symposium moderator. Yes, something was in the air.

The presentation before mine followed lunch and seemed rushed. It ended ten minutes early. Half the audience had left the room and were huddled in the corridors outside the main meeting room. I had anticipated the mid-afternoon slump phenomenon and had arranged catering to deliver trays of exotic chocolate confections during the break. I glanced at my watch as the parade of trays of three-dimensional spun sugar and chocolate confections soared through the auditorium on the uplifted hands of eight waiters. Members of the audience were mesmerized. As more people circled the food and others delicately dabbed the chocolate from the corners of their mouths, I started the video without waiting for the moderator to introduce me.

The popular music from 1962 filled the auditorium as shots of each country's coastlines filled the screen. They were views with recognizable features—resorts, city skylines, large tankers being loaded at ports of call, and military naval installations. Even though only the older installations were sampled, the sample size represented 30 locations.

"This is how your countries' naval installations looked 50 years ago Note the sea level readings at that time."

As the slides revealed the before sample to the rhythmic soul rock and Beatles songs, the crowd's attention was mine.

"Now let's look at a comparison of these same naval installations today, side by side." The slides repeated with photographs and sea levels to the background music of popular music of 2012. "The statistics are not startling, only inches higher in most places, but look at the effect of those inches. The Norfolk, VA facility floods when the tide and winds are right. Salt water gets in the steam lines where ships are moored. The problem is now. See for yourself."

The slides continued with the shift in music emphasizing the relative small gap in time. We all remember 1962 hits like they were yesterday.

"But we have heard presentations from several highly-regarded research institutions that the effects of global warming will change coastal areas even more. We have also learned that these computer models' accuracy depends on a number of variables, one of which is the rate at which carbon is released from the soil. My presentation is sponsored by the Etaq Center for Earth Sciences. Etaq has adjusted the computer model commonly used to project future sea level changes to incorporate that variable. Using the new model, we will next look at the current and projected sea level changes in 2017 and 2032. Watch as your country of interest is presented. Note the graph under the pictures that show changes in inches from 1962 to 2012, 2017 and 2032. The data and methodology details of our analysis can be found at www.ECES.org. We invite peer reviews of the papers documenting our work. Now, I will let the data speak."

At that point, the music volume rose as each country was examined in turn. The score was unfamiliar, but it captured the emotional effect of the tension building as data described increasing vulnerability. In every case for every country, military installations were rendered useless within twenty years. The power of the presentation was its translation of the data to images that showed the effects of even small increases in sea level on piers, access roads, important waterway networks, and military infrastructure. I suspected that the future shots were informed by time travel.

I then presented the cost in today's currency for addressing a four-inch rise in sea level at the Marine Corps facilities in Portsmouth, Virginia, and the cost basis for similar reconstruction of the nearby Norfolk Naval base. Once the concept of cost related to four-inch rise in sea levels was processed by the audience, I took them on a video tour of the sampled locations to see how that formula would apply to the sampled locations in their own countries. What followed was a visualization of the image of what sea levels would be at five- and ten-year intervals at specific locations and, for each, the cost of infrastructure upgrading where that would be possible. This process took time and could only have worked as a video. The images moved rapidly with music in the background. All eyes were on the screen. The seats were filled. The chocolate table was unattended.

The finale was the summary of economic costs to water-based shipping transport as a percentage of the country's GDP along with views of prime military installations flooded and were rendered useless. The music for these shots was perfect, providing an emotional tone of dread and doom that communicated our bleak future better than words.

As the last view grew smaller and smaller until it disappeared, I concluded the presentation. "Global warming's influence on sea-level change alone will render your naval capabilities useless in less than twenty years unless you sacrifice your economy to make the necessary infrastructure changes to keep pace with rises in sea level. In addition, your countries' ability to ship and receive goods via your seaports and rivers will also suffer and weaken your economies. That, ladies and gentlemen, is going to happen. Not in the far distant future as a Hollywood-worthy catastrophe movie, but between now and the next five years for many as a slow erosion of shorelines, backed-up sewer lines, street and bridge destruction from flash flooding, and the concomitant dramatic increase in deposits of mud and debris in ports from a burdened waterway network. Think about that. Five years speaks to tomorrow's elections and next week's stock market. I will now take questions."

The lights came up and there was a stirring of restless feet and shifting bodies seeking sanctuary from the overhead lights and the dreadful implications of the presentation. The Russian delegate spoke first. "I protest the invasion of our country's sovereignty to take secret photographs for the purpose of US propaganda."

"The photographs all come from the use of publicly-accessible satellite photography. You will find a description of our recording methods on our website." I replied succinctly and with that "Fiona" diva tone that I knew could be intimidating.

A Japanese delegate spoke, "The underlying assumption is that global warming is avoidable. Are you saying that it is caused by human intervention and we should do something about it?"

Before I could respond, a US delegate spoke, "If that is the case, may I remind the attendees that there are scientists who raise doubts about the existence of global warming as anything more than a natural cycle of climate change and our Congress remains divided on the issue."

"Name three. Scientists that is. I don't doubt there are numerous Congressmen holding that position." I replied directly to the US delegate.

"What?" he asked.

I repeated my request in a slow, measure tone. "Name three of the numerous scientists who don't believe that global warming is real or that it is not caused by human factors."

"Well, uh, I can't recall a particular name nor is that my purpose here to provide that information," he added.

"You are absolutely correct, Congressman Phillips. That is my purpose—to provide you with information. Take a look." I turned the video on to reveal a rolling list of names.

"These are the scientists who support the position that global warming is real and that it is a result of human behavior—something that we know is controllable." The list continued. "There are 928 names on this list." I waited until the last alphabetized name appeared.

"Now, here is the list of the scientists you referenced who hold the position that global warming is not an exceptional event along with those who think human behavior is not a factor in global warming."

Seven names appeared. "I believe you may have had one of these scientists in mind. Of these seven scientists, three conducted their research with funds from offshore bank accounts deposited by unknown sources. But I bet we could find out who made those deposits. Two others had their findings disputed by their peers and you can find the citations for those items in the list of references in our paper. The remaining two are preparing revisions to their former work to show a change in their position."

I continued. "My time is up, but I am sending this video to each delegate and have also posted it on YouTube. I invite you to share the paper in its entirety by downloading the file, "ECES Water," on our public website. Thank you for your attention during this presentation."

I slid the laptop in my briefcase and walked briskly from the podium to the nearest exit where my chauffer was waiting. He handed me my handbag and carried my raincoat on his arm. I followed him out to the curb and into the limo with the darkened glass. We were away into traffic before I relaxed my grip on the briefcase. We were in sight of the private air field before I relaxed my shoulders. We were airborne before I exhaled with a glass of Champagne in my hand.

By the time we landed in Los Angeles, I was struggling to remember how it had gone. Time seemed to stop and start as events progressed in slow motion or moved with image-blurring speed. How long had it been since I left the hotel? My watch told me three hours ago and here I was in front of the house in Malibu. I let myself in and returned the laptop to the desk, opened "ECES Water" on YouTube. The video already had over two million views. Posting it in each country's language was a brilliant tactic by someone as responses were coming in all over the world. The attendees of the conference would have a lot of explaining to do when they arrived home.

I checked Carlotta's e-mails. There were two.

"Well done, shithead," read one. I smiled at the inside joke and wondered who was responsible.

"Time and tide wait for no one," was the second. The Etaqs wanted me to hustle out of here.

I checked the tide tables for Malibu. The outgoing tide would peak at 10:05 p.m. I had three hours.

CHAPTER 35

The Etaq's rules of governance prohibit interference in the natural world of humans. By sending me back in time, they allowed me to make a presentation that, if it succeeds, would change how people respond to the threat of global warming. That I existed in that time naturally may be nothing more than a loophole for a possible defense, but better yet to leave no evidence that I was here at all. The Etaqs took a risk doing this to help us. We may need them to take more risks before it is over. Best to cover their hind-ends like they were my own.

I regretfully hung Carlotta's Chanel suits in the closet and compacted my trash. I left the money and credit cards in the desk drawer. Her passport with my picture and the laptop were stuffed in a small backpack. They would go with me.

As I watched the sunset from the deck one last time, I thought about all that had happened over the last few weeks and was filled with wonder. This has been the most enthralling adventure of my life. Aliens enlisted my help to slow climate change. Me, Fiona Campbell from Glover Gap! I was praised for my work by these brilliant creatures from another planet. How totally weird and fantastic is that? But I could not remain in this time. And it is likely that I could not leave it except by way of a wormhole that could be entered only as a subatomic particle. I would have to die to return to 2014 where I had been, where I hoped my friends were waiting for me. To remain here with my present consciousness and memories would be a violation of the Etaqs' ethical canons.

The computer clock was beeping 9:45 p.m. The tide was going out and I needed to be on it. I grabbed the backpack and took the stepped path down to the beach. The usually busy beach was deserted. I looked around for a sign of ECES's plan for putting me to sea and spotted a bright yellow one-person kayak resting a few yards beyond the reach of the surf. I tossed the backpack in, grabbed the paddle, and pulled the kayak to the water.

With one foot in and one out to push off, I took a deep breath of salty air and pushed and hopped until I had one foot in the icy water. The sudden shock of cold startled me for a second. One more push and the kayak was floating free. I paddled with a ferocity inspired by sheer panic as the sound of breaking surf ahead thundered in my ears. I dipped the paddle on alternating sides as I had learned that summer in the Catskills. But that had been on a lake in daylight with people around—a peaceful float past ducks and loons. This excursion, however, was charged with adrenaline born of fear. I was afraid that I would turn over if I didn't hit the surf straight on, afraid that the kayak would fill with water as surf washed over me, afraid that I wouldn't make it out of sight of the people who typically partied on the beach and might show up any minute, afraid that I would screw this up—this one last hard thing that must be done to finish my assignment. My breathing came in gasps as I pointed the kayak straight across the white frothing surf and a voice in my head screamed, "Paddle like a motherfucker, Fiona!"

I leaned forward and dug the paddle in deep, pulled hard against it with my feet braced in the bow of the little boat, switched sides and dug down for another. For a time, it seemed the kayak wasn't moving. Then the ominous roar of the surf ahead broke through the ragged breathing in my ears. I picked up my pace to make sure that the kayak would form a right angle with the ferocious white froth. I ducked my head, and pulled on the paddles, shifting my hands as I traded sides. Bile and seawater choked me, but I was through the crested wave and moving fast across a swell with no fight in it. I kept paddling until the noise of the surf was fading and I was at least 150 yards from shore. I paused, paddle resting across my lap, my hands trembling from exertion. The tide was taking me out to sea, but I continued to paddle to speed it along. I needed to be far away, so far away that no evidence of my visit would be found near the house.

I must have collapsed from exhaustion because I came to later slumped forward with my head resting on the kayak's hull. The paddle was gone. The shoreline was now an indistinct border of lights. This should be far enough. Using my feet to scoot the backpack to where I could reach it, I took out the laptop and passport and dropped them in. They scarcely made a ripple. I slipped on the now-empty backpack for warmth.

Well, here I am. Nothing left to do. I could bask in my successful completion of a job well done, but I am too cold, wet, and hungry to bask. Blisters torture my hands each time the salt water finds them. I tuck them under my armpits and return my head to rest on the fiberglass hull of the kayak. The backpack shelters me from the leeward wind. Exhaustion overtakes me as the swells move me up and down, like a tiny doll in a toy boat. A vibration in the hull fills my head with a humming sound that soon surrounds me. Mother is singing me to sleep. I smile as thoughts of Valerie telling off the Etaqs came to mind. She was doing her best imitation of me. I can't wait to die and get home to my pod. So much to learn and experience.

Just like the first time I died, I could look down and see my dead self as it sunk with the kayak and disappeared. My AtCon glowed a cheery pink. I was looking forward to learning how to travel in time. My thoughts went to the library and today's date— September 14th—and the year 2014. The rest I left to the Etaqs.

The End

ABOUT THE AUTHOR

A. Lee Bruno is retired from a career in social science research and lives in Prince George's County, Maryland, where this novel is set. The magnolia tree featured in this book is a tree she planted when she moved to the Washington, D.C. area from Pensacola, Florida. Her favorite people to hang out with are her children and grandchildren who are funny, smart, and full of love. When she is not writing, she is working on a new way to keep the deer from eating her landscaping.

Lee writes feminist fiction from the perspective of a woman who has lived through many generational changes. She draws on her 75 years and training in psychology to create character-driven fiction that crosses over all the genres. Other books include:

Pensacola Reset. After her 15-year abusive marriage ends, a woman returns home to figure out the rest of her life and find a cure for loneliness. First, she is seduced by the beaches and, then, by a man 10 years younger. http://amzn.to/1o3rcyn

Abnorm Chronicles: Two Queens and a Rook. Three women and a psychopathic assassin team up to take down Public Enemy #1 in this spin-off of Marcus Sakey's SF thriller.

BEFORE YOU GO:

Review Now That I'm Dead here: http://amzn.to/1QafCb4

And share your thoughts about these books with the author Leebrunobooks@yahoo.com and your Facebook and Twitter buddies. Be the first on your street to discover a new novelist with a distinctive style.

Made in the USA
Columbia, SC
27 June 2021

40780945R00134